GOOFBANG VALUE DAZE

Also by JULIAN F. THOMPSON

GOOFBANG VALUE DAZE

JULIAN F. THOMPSON

SCHOLASTIC
HARDCOVER

Scholastic Inc.
New York

Copyright © 1989 by Julian F. Thompson.
All rights reserved. Published by Scholastic Inc.
SCHOLASTIC HARDCOVER is a registered trademark of Scholastic Inc.

No part of this publication may be reproduced in whole or in part, or stored
in a retrieval system, or transmitted in any form or by any means, electronic,
mechanical, photocopying, recording, or otherwise, without written permission of the publisher. For information regarding permission, write to Scholastic
Inc., 730 Broadway, New York, NY 10003.

Library of Congress Cataloging-in-Publication Data

Thompson, Julian F.
    Goofbang value daze / Julian F. Thompson.
        p.   cm.
    Summary: In a futuristic community set under a huge dome, a riot erupts
at a high school when students protest the school directors' authoritarian
measures.
    ISBN 0-590-41946-3
    [1. High schools — Fiction.   2. Schools — Fiction.   3. Science fiction.]
    I. Title.
PZ7.T371596GO   1989
[Fic] — dc19   88-23893
                                                                    CIP
                                                                     AC

12 11 10 9 8 7 6 5 4 3 2 1   9/8 0 1 2 3 4/9

                    Printed in the U.S.A.   37

                First Scholastic printing, April 1989

*In memory of Dead Horse. And for Polly,
the love of both our happy lives.*

1
EVERYBODY TALKS

What you are about to read is a test. Do not turn this page or, worse yet, close this book. This is just a test.

I couldn't imagine anyone having a better relationship with their parents than I do.

What you just read was only a test. It isn't the sort of thing I'd say — although it happens to be true — because I can't stand the sort of person who makes ridiculous, unconditional statements like that when he doesn't even know you. I also wouldn't want you to think that this is one of those totally wholesome books in which the effects of hard work and a close-knit family pay off in national heroism of some sort. Or that I'm one of those neurotic, self-satisfied little prigs who'll never make a happy marriage because he'll never find a "gal" who measures up to "Mom."

I *think* I get along with my parents this well because they know that everything is serious (but also goof around a lot), they act the way they say they want *me* to (and thus keep nag time to a minimum), and they don't pretend they have the total answer book for all the major questions (and so have faith, unlimited).

So ends the test. And storytelling starts. Believe it. Please.

When I was ten — six years ago — my father came storming into the house one rainy Monday afternoon. It was right after the Masters. The Masters *golf* tournament? The one they have down in Augusta every year? That one. The trouble was, he hated driving in the rain, and it was pouring. But I was glad to see him anyway; he'd been away from home a week.

My mother wrapped her arms around his neck and kissed him in a way I'd only just begun to understand a little. But which also made me laugh, although I didn't yet know why.

"It's meant to be real nice on Wednesday," I said, when they had got unstuck, she laughing, too.

"You should have seen it yesterday," she added. "It was *really* pouring yesterday, right, Gabe?"

"Young Gabriel, Patricia," my father said to us, "Mark Twain had it right: Everybody *talks* about the weather, but nobody ever *does* anything about it."

I think I thought he meant Mark *Trail*, but still I smiled and nodded. At ten, I wasn't old enough to say, "True, true."

The next year, though, was the year they built the dome over the entire city of Dustin, all of our hometown. It was a quarter sphere two miles across, transparent, made of glass, glass cloth and huge aluminum and stainless steel trusses and supports. The top of the dome was well over a thousand feet above the ground, and its bottom rim was more than five hundred feet up, so Dustin, from a distance (or an airplane) looked as if they'd put a big, wide lid on it. Air circulated freely underneath the thing, but neither rain nor snow came down inside, of course.

I never threw the dome up at my father, or sued him for corrupting the credulity of a minor by telling me that true, true thing that soon turned out to be completely false. But from that year on, I think, my innocence was out the window. Like my parents, I henceforth both believed and said that anything was possible — including stuff I absolutely "knew" was not.

When I was twelve, for instance, I told my father (who was skipping the Bob Hope Desert Classic) that it was all right, that I *knew* my real father had been a black colonel in the United States Air Force, and my real mother a Vietnamese nurse. I didn't think anything of the sort, of course.

"What?" he said. "You do? But how about the way you look? You tried a mirror, lately?"

I hadn't, but I didn't have to; I knew exactly what I'd see. A brown-haired white kid on the skinny side, taller than average, with a big head and an almost perpetual smile, and his shirt coming out of his pants.

"Looks don't have that much to do with it," I said. "Colors do weird things, like when you mix two different ones together. Yellow and blue make green. Black and yellow *could* make white, or sort of tan anyway, like me. Especially if you've got white mixed in with the black to start with, the way you almost always do in America, from what my teacher says. But anyway, it really doesn't matter whose I am. Birth is just an accident, Lafountain said. And you and Mom have been just great to me."

My father — Craig Podesta is his name — just shook his head. He's a Phi Beta Kappa graduate of Duke University, where he double-majored in physics and psychology, *tripled* if you want to count my mother, who was also in psychology and single at the time. For the past sixteen years he's gone around on the professional golf tour, not playing — he couldn't break a hundred with that loopy swing he has — but helping real good players with their putting. Using his understanding of the laws of physics and of optics (or is that part of physics?) and his awareness of the ways that mind and matter interact, he'd become (he swore to me that this was so) the greatest putter of all time. And true to the motto on his business cards ("Drive for show, putt for dough"), he tooled around the country in a white Bugatti and earned two hundred grand a year off bets in putting contests with his once and future pupils. His formal lessons were a mere four hundred for the hour, and well worth it, everybody said. But no one ever got as good as he was, everybody noticed.

"I'm glad you feel that way," he told me now. "And we can say the same. You've really turned out pretty well, whoever you are. You see him more than I do, Pattie. Isn't he, in general, a source of pride and joy, a solace in your early middle age?"

"Absolutely." My mother walked around behind my chair and put her hands down on my shoulders in the standard mother-offspring way. I suspended my attack on the French toast.

"I think he may *be* ours," she said. "He puts his pants on one leg at a time, and ketchup on his hot dogs, same as we do. But still. Weird things take place in hospitals, especially in nurseries. Computers aren't foolproof by a long shot. Like, if you're a dyslexic nurse in a hurry, there isn't that much difference between six thousand six hundred and eighteen and S-I-ninety-nine, you know. Hit a few wrong buttons and one kid gets a second bath and the other one is packed and flying to Topeka with two strangers. I heard they found this cocker spaniel with a baby's wristlet on, one time, just walking down the aisle between the bassinets. *Probably* an accident, but, well, who knows?"

"That reminds me." And I craned my neck around so I could see her. "What makes an IUD work, anyway? I told Lafountain I'd find out."

Because my father drove a white Bugatti and my mother sort of ran a clinic, people came to think I knew things, or had access, anyway. "Ask Podesta"

5

was a not uncommon cry at Dustin Junior High, and one that I did nothing to discourage, that's for sure. It wasn't going to be my looks or jump shot that'd get me human contacts of the sort we all desire. "Everybody can contribute something to the cabin," this counselor of mine had said the summer that my parents sent me off to camp and took their shot at Europe. What I can offer to my fellow beasts is information, curiosity and caring. Sometimes too much caring; I'm not kidding.

Four years later, when I was sixteen (as I am still, now) it came time once again to elect the three school directors of the city of Dustin. The election was usually a pretty low-key affair. The different candidates would run small ads in the *Dustin Times*, and one or two of them would build a car-roof sign and seem to drive around a lot. And a couple of weeks before the election, there'd be a candidates' "forum" in the high school gym that about forty people would attend, mostly relatives and busybodies.

But this year, for the first time that my parents could remember, there were three candidates who seemed to be running more or less as an entry. And in addition to ads in the paper and signs on all three of their cars, they posted handbills all over town — on poles, on sticks in people's lawns, in any window (store *or* home) that owners would allow them into.

The handbills — they were really cardboard signs — had pictures of the terrible trio on them (Dr. Fabian Leeds, T. Hank Nevins and Beatrice Teagle), and they also had this slogan:

Education for America:
        *L*earning
        *O*rder
        *V*alues
        *E*xcellence
            for all our children.

After I'd read that about a million times, I couldn't stand it anymore. Something snapped. I wrote a letter to the editor of *Dust Devils*, which is the Dustin High School paper. Here it is, in its historical entirety.

To the editor:

Pooh-pooh, pooh-pooh, pooh-pooh, poop. That's this chile's reaction to the Leeds-Nevins-Teagle landscape blots. "Education for America"? Humbug! "*LOVE* for all our children"? Millsap! Education, as anyone who's ever sucked up any knows, is a totally mysterious process. If anyone knew how to make it happen, everybody would. Right? Right. End of argument. Good-bye.

Gabriel Podesta, Junior Class

P.S. Berke Breathed might make a good school director, but offhand I can't think of anybody else.
P.P.S. Certainly not any of this mad triad.

7

P.P.P.S. Which, in (Murphy's) law-abiding Dustin, is almost certain to win. In a mudslide.

"Under previous administrations, everybody talked about the low pressure system of abdicative adult apathy," said Dr. Leeds, "interfacing with the cold front of the text-and-teacher-sponsored class-room value void, but no one's ever *done* thing one about it."

No reference to either of the Marks, you'll notice.

The school directors were having their first public meeting since the election which, of course, they won — won *big* — just as certain pundits had predicted. It was being held in the faculty cafeteria (which seemed significant to me), and Leeds and them were leaning on a table which I believe, in normal circumstances, was the place where lunch meats lay.

At forty-four years old and six foot two, Fabian Leeds, M.D., maintained his weight at one-four-oh, his body fat at 2.6%. His head-skin — interrupted only by a fringe of rusty hair — fit so tight that I could almost read his mind, I thought. And where my father kept *his* Phi Beta Kappa key in a pants pocket and used it to repair the ball and spike marks that showed up on greens, Leeds wore his hanging from his left earlobe. Actually, once you got used to it, and possibly because he always wore a gray or dark blue suit with a vest and tie, it didn't look all that weird.

"And that's plain fact," said T. Hank Nevins from

the chair to Leeds's right. He gave himself a few approving pats on the back of his full and lustrous head of steel-gray hair. He was wearing cowboy boots and blue jeans and a western shirt, and you could absolutely tell he saw himself as just "a real good Joe."

T. Hank was the owner of a statewide chain of hair and skin and exercise salons called Byoutifactions. My mom told me he'd inherited the first one, Katrinka Nevins's Beauty Nook ("Trink Nevins for Little Curls") from *his* mom and had just gone on from there. His two grown kids were ten years out of school (and state, in fact) and were, Mom said, in a nude ice revue and on a touring donkey softball team, respectively. She believed T. Hank saw his school directorship as a good political springboard, the start-up of his number-two career. Having learned (in number one) what women thought they wanted for themselves and for their children, he could promise that to them from every podium, and more. Me, I had no trouble believing that this superbly groomed (yet folksy) airhead was one of the most promising faces — or if not that, *mouths* — in all of this-here domed metropolis.

"Mmmm," said Beatrice Teagle, thoughtfully; she was seated at the doctor's left. Homemaker and columnist ("Bea-Lines" every other Wednesday, in the *Times*), Mrs. Teagle was a well-known quantity, a spokesma'am for the "old school" and the "good old days," when "rights" were (simply) just the opposite of "wrongs." Here's something that I think I've noticed: Whenever someone starts a sentence with "I guess I'm of the old school on . . . blah-blah," the chances are real good they're going to say they're for some deal they know darn well they ought to be ashamed of.

"It's promises-to-keep time, friends," T. Hank jumped back in to say, looking left to right around the room. In addition to myself, there were about eighty other people there. That was scary, in and of itself; the thing that made it worse was most of them began to nod each time his Hank-ness moved his lips.

"There's wars just waiting to be won," came out between them, now. "On 'good-enough' and 'no-can-do' and 'let-it-run-its-course' and 'what-if-they-don't-like-it' and. . . ."

I crouched and slunk out a side door. Face it, "Gabriel Podesta" might have been the next words in that sentence.

2
VALUE DAYS

My parents tell me that while it was going up, the dome was one of those rare ideas that almost everybody speaks in favor of, although for different reasons. Selfish ones? Who knows? But even I was what you'd call a booster, at the time. Of course it's also fair to say that having only reached the big one-one (I'm talking years, not beauty standards, here) my judgments sometimes showed their age. Anything was "neat" if it was big enough, or made my smelly yellow slicker obsolete, or looked as if it might belong in *Star Wars* movies. Big Lid qualified, in all three cases.

In any case, the dome put Dustin on the map and in the news; it covered us and all three networks covered *it*. Before, our town was "just outside of Ellington," a sort of not-our-kind-of-person neighbor in the eyes of Ellingtonians — the type that has loud arguments, competing with an AM radio, and keeps a brown Impala (with its body getting crispy) in the driveway. Now, however, we were out there on the cutting edge of — possibly — *tomorrow*. "Is this the city of the future?" asked Dan Rather, staring at the nation's living rooms and trying not to smile.

Before, a lot of Dustin homes were solid wooden shapes dating from the 1920s, and looking like the ones on Boardwalk and Park Place, or Marvin Gardens, five bedrooms and a bath. We'd had three mills in town when they were built, but as they closed most people drove to Ellington to work, where all the better stores and lawyers were.

In five years' time and with the dome, however, everything got changed around. People from all over, even Ellington, came and bought the houses and remodeled them. Soon, there weren't many roofers left in town, but tub and vanity and toilet sales went through the ceiling, anyway, and former mudrooms got new floors, made out of ornamental tiles. Porches were rebuilt and bushes added, with more privacy in mind; dormer and those bay-type bubble windows popped from sidings and from roofs like zits. Wine-and-cheese and lingerie boutiques with names like *Prosit* and Xilly's took the place of candy stores, and a lot of younger, Saabier lawyers came to town and started taking business from the ones in Ellington. The streets (at least) were never slick and slippery in Dustin and, thanks to the Dustin Downtown Master Plan, you didn't have a lot of trouble finding parking. People started driving in from Ellington to work in shops and lawyers' offices, and even Dustin High.

Who knows how much the dome had to do with the school directors' election? We live in times when anything gets blamed for everything. I read that acid rain was caused by lack of fiber in the diet of the trilobites, back when fossil fuels were being made. I think that although I agree with my parents when they say that nothing that happens in town these days is altogether *un*affected by Big Lid, I tend to see the dome as more of a "symptom" than a "cause."

We love to use those words, Dori and Lafountain and myself, especially since Mr. Varney Poole, our social studies teacher, began to say them almost every day of our lives, it seemed like.

At times, we wondered which one Varney was, just kidding.

"The thing I ask myself," said Dori Fabb, one day, "is whether Varney makes coming to school feel like those last fifteen seconds before you throw up, or whether he's just part of the general weirdness. Oliver L. North in mufti. Younger and more of a stay-at-home, of course."

Dori doesn't look as if she knew words like "mufti," or names like "Oliver L. North." Going by appearances, you'd put her down as strong on "silk charmeuse" and cousin Calvin K. Here she is: a wide-eyed mop-head, brown-eyed blonde, who takes a tan and freckles. She's also five foot seven, lithe and limber, and appears entirely free of cares and inhibitions — also maybe even underwear — although, in fact, she has a pretty standard 1980s set of each, so far as I can tell. My father, who's been known to show a corny side, once said she was "cute as a whole drawerful of buttons," and you can throw in zippers, hooks and eyelets, drawstrings, even Velcro closures while you're at it, they being all the things that Dori made the average ten-fingered guy in the world think about undoing. Most people thought she was a nut case, too, on account of who she'd chosen as her boyfriend. Hint: a brown-haired white kid on the skinny side, taller than average, with a big head and an almost perpetual smile, and his shirt still coming out of his pants.

The two questions I've been asked the most, to this point in my life, are: "Could I borrow — uh, you know — your homework?" and "What the hell's she see in you?"

My answers are: "I'm sorry," and a shrug (respectively).

Liar. I wasn't — and of course I know.

I can almost hear Lafountain say, "Oh, yeah?"

Lafountain always gets his 2¢ in. He's my other closest friend and he spends a lot of time with me and Dori, playing a sort of conversational free-safety, stepping in and intercepting things we've thrown at one another.

"The thing I ask *my*self," he said, right after Dori'd raised that facetious question about Varney Poole, "and then the stars up above, is why must *you* be" — he clasped his hands in front of where he thought his heart was — "a teenager in luh-huv?"

Lafountain wasn't really serious. Oh, he might have lusted after Dori in his heart — who wouldn't? I'm pretty sure that Varney does; President Carter

14

probably would have, as would Dion and the Belmonts, if I know anything about musicians. But Lafountain, simple as he is, will sometimes say one thing to mean another. He thinks that's being smart. In this case, I believe he was pointing out how complicated life can be for people in our age group.

Want proof? Well, take a letter. Here's a list of complications we endure, ones starting only with the letter D:

> Dome,
> Directors (School), and
> Dustin High.
> Drugs and alcohol, and sexual
> Desire.

And starting on a certain Thursday morning:

> Dumb idea.

Varney Poole was not entirely typical of the young male teachers at the high school. First of all, he wasn't certified. But he also didn't have that teacher's look about him, what Lafountain called the what-the-fuck-but-I-can-help-you stare. He was a squarish, clean-cut-looking guy who tended toward tweed jackets, hiking boots and soft-soft-looking wide-wale corduroys. He also perched atop his desk, legs dangling, or stood against the windows, on the side, one elbow on the sill, as if it were a mantelpiece. He hardly ever wrote things on the board; his spelling and his penmanship were dreadful.

"Don't flip," he said to us that memorable Thursday, "but in this course, this year, we're going to borrow not a concept, but a label, from the world of merchandising. From Mad Ave. You've heard of 'Value Days' at Kmart and the like, I'm sure. . . ." He looked around the room, a big grin on his small, but friendly, face.

"Mad Ave," pronounced Madav, was where old Varney wanted us to think he would have been if he hadn't gotten drunk one night and been shanghaied aboard this ship of fools, the SS *Dustin High*.

I glanced at Dori. She was staring over to the side at him, looking totally confounded, as if he'd said all that in Urdu.

"*K*mart, Mr. Poole?" she asked. She was pretending she was taking notes. "You spell that with a 'c'? 'Q-u'? Is that a *store*? In Ellington, or something?"

"Right," said Varney. "Sure, Dorinda. We *know* you only shop at *Lauren's*, with Brooke *Shields*. . . ."

Dori grinned at him, and Varney blushed. She'd suckered him again. It was a little game they played, and Varney always lost.

Don't get me wrong. Varney Poole and I are friends. The guy's an optimist, he really is; that's one thing I like about him. Possibly he isn't brilliant, but we learn stuff in his class because he sells us on the caring, trying parts of learning, and we like him. He isn't mean; he doesn't pull a lot of rank on kids, or act as if he isn't human. He admits that he has weaknesses, emotions, just like us. The first time I asked him if he'd like to come to dinner at my house, he didn't make a joke or act suspicious. He just said,

"Absolutely. Sure. What time?" He came at six and we have stuffed the guy, fortnightly, ever since.

"But anyway . . ." he'd started up again, "on Mondays, all semester — and probably the next one, too — we're going to take a look at values in America. The ones we have and why we have them."

He beamed around the room. We were holding our applause.

"Uh, yes?" he said. "Dorinda?" Dori had her hand up, once again.

"When you say the ones 'we' have," she said, "does that mean you and the rest of the *teachers*, or the members of this *class*, the people in this *town*, or what?" Dori paused; Varney blinked. "Or do you mean your *generation*, maybe, as compared to other ones? And when you say 'values,' are you talking about stuff like *abortions*?" She paused again. "And I have a follow-up."

I looked back at Varney. He was blinking very rapidly, digesting.

"No. No, no, no — not abortions," he replied. He'd jumped into a safety zone, he thought. "I'm talking oatmeal here, a peanut butter sandwich, apple pie. The basic goods that build up happy lives and good relationships. Examples: thoughtfulness and honesty, fairness and fidelity, self-discipline, respect for law and order. Stuff like that. Mainstream, high-tops, button jeans." Varney smiled at Dori, giving her a happy nod. Then he looked around the room, speaking to us all.

"A lot of us," he said, "heck, most of you, have learned these things at home, I'm sure. The *do's* and *don't's*. American basics. Unless a person's really

17

clear about the basics, he hasn't got a . . . uh, a *basis* for the judgments that he has to make on . . . things. On abortion, like Dorinda said. Just like in anything, you have to walk before you can . . . uh, *fly*. So."

Varney took a big, deep breath. I think he knew he hadn't said the last part just exactly right, but he probably figured no one noticed; we tended not to, as a class. He looked back at Dori.

"You had a follow-up?" he said.

Dori shook her head. "Not anymore," she said. "I have a statement, though."

"What's that?" said Varney, stupidly.

"Let us pray," she said.

Varney laughed; I laughed; she laughed; the whole class laughed. We shouldn't have. We should have prayed, like Dori said.

3
DO'S AND DON'T'S,
PART ONE

Drink your milk.
Don't cry.
Look both ways before you cross the street.
Stog bugging me/him/her/them/everyone.
Change your underwear.
Don't look at me that way.
Clean up the mess you made.
Turn off TV.
Say "please" and "thank you" and "excuse me."
Never take a thing that isn't yours.
Try a little harder.
Don't be silly.

4
STANCHION PARTY

"Don't!" and "Eek!" shrieked Dori Fabb, her eyes as wide as if she'd just seen someone putting on a bright red leather miniskirt with penny loafers. The fact is, she was looking at me, and no one else that mattered heard her. Lafountain was right there, of course.

But the music was real loud around the stanchion where the flares had been set out. Here and there, around us on the slope, a few grills glowed. I thought I got a whiff of broiling beefalo, and also (maybe) breast of public pigeon.

"Don't!" squealed Dori, once again.

I beamed at her, delighted — *flattered*. Dori was standing with her back to a tree, and I had just produced the can of beer I'd hidden in my jacket pocket. I'd also seized it by the top, as if I were about to rip the thing in half, the way that L.C. Greenwood does, on one Lite beer commercial.

Oh, yes. Her cry was music to the ears of someone who's been known to have real trouble with the ketchup bottle top.

I nodded, happy to give in.

"All right, all *right*," I said. I dropped the can back in my pocket. "But if I can't have beer, that just leaves you-know-what." I bounced my eyebrows up and down, and grinned. "So how about a little game of hide-the-ferret? Hmmm?" I leered and reached for her.

"Oh, o-right," she said, surprisingly. She used her cheerful-slattern's whine. "I s'pose we might as well. You gentlemen have got to have your bit o' fun." She wrapped her arms around my neck. "Comes from 'avin' moats and *gargoyles*, right?"

"Hey, break it up, you guys," Lafountain said. "Let's show a little common decency, okay? There's people here less fortunate than you, you know."

That almost had to be the case, given all the bodies in the neighborhood. We were at a Stanchion Party, as most everybody called them, now that there'd been three. But this was much the biggest one, by far. *Of course* that made me nervous (he remarks, speaking from the top of old Mount Hindsight).

I know exactly how the darn things started. I was there — Dori and myself and you-know-who. He even had a date that night, with Leah Presto, and the four of us were sitting at a redwood table beside the take-out window of Marie's Noovel Kweezeen, finishing our cold-duck-salad sandwiches. Other

21

people were at other tables, all around us.

"Stars! I need to see some stars, some naked stars," somebody said. Possibly Lafountain. He didn't mean Tom Cruise or Lisa Bonet, either.

And everybody said, "Oh, yeah."

Well, no one in the group had access to a car, and so we had to stop and figure out where we could go that wasn't miles away, but also would be seminice and semiprivate. Sound familiar? Sort of like the Universal Age-Group Problem? Dori's father told me once that youth is wasted on the young. Here's what I think: Privacy is wasted on the old.

Lafountain had a great idea. We'd walk out on the jogging path by Roosevelt Avenue, then angle off it onto the former landfill access road that now was blocked to automotive traffic by these huge wooden pilings driven deep into its concrete surface, more or less four feet apart. Down that road there was a gully that the town had dumped in years before, but which now was overgrown with trees and bushes. A little bosky wood it was, rooted in the garbage of the past.

Just above the gully was a stanchion, one of those immense supports that held up Dustin's dome. That meant when you walked down a ways from *it*, into the wooded former dump, you were, in fact, *outside* — in the world of Mother Nature, bathed in starlight, out from under, free.

I think that's why the Stanchion Parties got to be a thing. I told this to Lafountain, that I saw them as a symbol of our need to . . . well, *escape*. I said that maybe kids were drawn to Stanchion Parties by the sort of urges that the great explorers and

22

adventurers had felt, guys like F. Magellan, Polo, M., or what's-his-name, the first one to go faster than the speed of sound.

"Jimi Hendrix," said Lafountain. "Yeah, I think that's right. I'm pretty sure it's someone dead."

I rolled my eyes and changed the subject. Lafountain likes to goof on me when I get serious. I know he gets a little tired of the way I look for symbols, seek out explanations. I also like it when there isn't any explanation, though. When there is Mystery. "I relate to mystery," I told Lafountain once, while we were eating lunch at school. "Good," he answered, "here," pushing these two meatballs off his plate and onto mine.

But still, I love to babble theories at the guy, try out different words, connect the stuff I learn at school to things I get from home, or just think up myself. Sometimes what I say turns out to sound like utter bullshit, and I drop it from my repertoire. That's how I learned to not say certain words out loud, like "repertoire." Lafountain never holds my less successful stuff against me, I don't think. Possibly he pays less close attention than I like to think he does.

Anyway — the parties did catch on. But mostly just with local high school kids; you didn't see a lot of Texans at the things, or raceboat drivers in the import-export biz. As to what the kids were doing there, they would mostly claim they were "relaxing," although it's fair to say that some of them were getting all excited doing things that adults had advised them not to do or, in the case of Dustin High, forbidden them.

That had happened three weeks earlier. There'd been a notice that was read in every homeroom, and that, furthermore, was posted in the hallways, and that (finally) was pinned on everybody's jacket to take home.

5
NOTICE

Any student who uses or possesses alcohol, or nonprescription drugs, on school property or at any school-related activity shall be suspended for ten days for the first offense and, if there be a second offense, shall be dismissed from Dustin High School.

R.D. Morehead, Principal

6
REACTIONS

"What the hell is that supposed to mean?" asked Deano Dobbins. A bunch of us were mashed against the b-board, right outside the Office. " '. . . any school-related activity . . .'? Like what?"

"Like athletic events at another school, for one thing," said Mouse Barini, who is on the soccer team. "I know that Coach gets really pissed when he sees kids partying up in the stands, laughing and carrying on, when we're all keeping training rules and out there busting our humps for the school. He thinks that gives the town of Dustin, like, a real bad name."

"*I've* seen you guys play though, rodent," Deano said, "and I've got news for you. It's not the people in the stands that's blackening the name of Dustin soccer."

"Very funny, Deano," Mousie said, "but maybe

if we had a little more support. . . ."

I'd tuned their conversation out and turned away. Earlier, I'd done my own analysis, with Dori and Lafountain, also in the hall.

"Why this? Why now?" I asked.

"Huh?" Dorinda said. "Have you been in a coma? Does the phrase 'national emergency' ring a bell? How about an 'all-out war' on something? Nancy *Reagan*, maybe?" She wrinkled up her nose. "Some 'priceless natural resource' *you* are."

"Anyone who says he has to drink or smoke in school has got a problem," said Lafountain. "Pills, I'm not so sure."

"What?" said Dori. "What? You're saying. . . ? Wait. Bad as it may be, you can't tell me that someone has to. . . ."

"*Kidding*," said Lafountain, and he winked at me.

"Still," I said. "I don't see the situation here as having changed so much. Like, lately." I opened up my locker, reached into my stash of peanut butter cups.

"And you would know?" said Dori. "Changed since when? Since kindergarten? Gimme one of those. You didn't see those people on the teeter-totters, yesterday?" I shrugged and fed her.

"They *ought* to be suspended," said Lafountain. "What they are is just a total waste of time. Me, if I was Principal, I'd get 'em out of here. Bye-bye." He flapped his fingers up and down. "I wouldn't miss those bozos. Kick a little ass — why not?"

"Well, possibly be-*cause* those kids have got a *prob*-lem," Dori said. "Possibly, they need some help and understanding — *treatment*, Boo-Boo. Very special counseling. You think you'll never have a problem you can't deal with by yourself?" Lafountain shook his head. "You don't think that's possible?" He pooched his lips way out, like Mick, and shook his head again. "You want to know the truth? You've got one now, right now." She grinned at him, triumphantly.

"Uh-uh. The hell I do. What is it?" said Lafountain. "I don't have a problem. You're just trying to bluff me." He pointed at the middle button of his new Hawaiian shirt. "I am the master of my fate, Dorinda."

"Ha-ha, thinks you," said Dori. "You've got a biggie, Fontski, kid yourself. But I'm not telling it to *you*. I'll whisper it to Gabe, and he can be the judge if I'm not right."

Dori put her lips right by my ear and barely breathed the following: "Pretend you found a little severed *something* in this soda you were drinking — "

"Eee*ooh*!" I said, and made a face, recoiling.

"See?" said Dori, proudly. "Even Gabe-y thinks that it's disgusting. . . ."

"I see what both of you are saying," I threw in. "No one has the right to mess up someone else's education, but it's still important that — "

"Hey, never mind that stuff," Lafountain said. "What did Dori tell you, anyway?" He turned to her. "You liar." Then back to me. "Come on. Hey, Gabe, are you my friend or what?"

"I know that Morehead's got to look as if he's trying," Dori said to me, "but what does *he* know, really about — "

28

"You don't drink *or* smoke," Lafountain said to her. "That makes you just as bad as Morehead, Leeds, or anyone like that. Mrs. Teagle smokes Virginia Slims, at least. I saw her. But you, you'll never understand the problem."

" '*If there be*' is something Leeds would say, not Morehead," I tossed out. "In the notice, it said 'if there be . . .' blah-blah."

"Will you make up your mind?" said Dori to Lafountain. "One minute all you say is 'kick 'em out.' Now you're calling what they've got a 'problem.' That's something else that's wrong with you. You've got no standards or opinions. You're just one mass of problems, my young friend."

At the end of that, she deepened down her voice and dropped her right hand on his shoulder, squeezing. Mr. Morehead does that, sometimes, when he chats you down a hall.

7
STANCHION PARTY (2)

Dancing was a thing you did at Stanchion Parties. Therefore, Dori Fabb, participant, good sport, had dragged our four left feet (two of mine, a couple of Lafountain's) into a throbbing, swaying mass of friends, acquaintances, and looks-familiar-but's. Some members of that group appeared a little wasted, but no one that I saw was being violent or obnoxious. Basically, the scene was one that specimens my age describe as "fun."

Dori Fabb can actually *dance*. She gets right into bouncing, grinding with the beat, a big grin on her face, enjoying it because she's good at it, I claim. Meanwhile, I, to my disgust/regret, stay cautious, uncommitted, looking stiff and breakable, I always think. I *hate* me on the dance floor. I jerk around (both meanings), look at Dori, make some semi-singing sounds, and get distinctly hot.

All three of us were sweating when we finally left the dance space, arm-in-arm. We were heading for a twin hibachi, partway down the slope. Donald Cremin was providing coals and cutlery, we had brought the bratwurst and a loaf of deli rye, plus condiments. Salivation City.

Donald was a year ahead of us in school — a weirdo, and we liked him. Instead of blankets and the like, he always brought this small, inflatable canoe to outdoor parties. And, usually, a different date; tonight, she was a stranger and voluptuous. I think her name was Sandi.

"You want to know the closest thing to a Club Med on all the *Côte de* Dustin?" he inquired of me once. "It's Cap'n Cremin's little love boat, boy."

But as I said, he never seemed to keep a girlfriend very long. When I asked Lafountain why he thought that was, he said he bet that girls got "C-sick," kissing Donald in his love boat. That was pretty witty, for Lafountain.

By the time the three of us had joined the two of them, the coals were perfect. Bingo: five fat little sausages, sizzling and bursting as we turned them, smelling really great. Typically impatient, Dori was the first to grab the tongs and take hers off. She wrapped it in a piece of rye and reached across me and inside the rubber boat for ketchup.

As she did so, I took out that can of beer that I'd been brandishing before, and thoughtlessly — or "tragically," as Dori later said — snapped down the pop-top. Two things happened, right away.

The first one was the obvious. Beer shot out, all

31

over Dori's reaching arm and shoulder. Then it foamed straight up and showered me. Of course I *quickly* yanked the nasty thing away and aimed it toward the empty darkness — but the damage had been done.

The second thing was not my fault — unless you want to put the blame on me for starting Stanchion Parties to begin with. A highly amplified and unmistakably authoritarian voice boomed out from up above us:

"ALL RIGHT, YOU KIDS," it said, "THE PARTY'S OVER. THIS IS CAPTAIN ARCHER OF THE TOWN POLICE. EVERYBODY STAY RIGHT WHERE YOU ARE. THE OFFICERS WILL TAKE. . . ."

At about that point, perhaps fifteen or twenty of those huge long flashlights that a cop will always have, clicked on, making one big arc around the stanchion, pointing out in our direction, down the slope. And at that point, too, a lot of us young party animals took off, including this kid here, and Dori, and Lafountain. Captain Donald stayed and went down with his ship, and Sandi with him, never to be seen again. I'm not real sure what happened to the bratwursts.

It wasn't guilt that put wings on our heels, I don't believe. Oh, I guess we realized there might be something wrong — unlawful, even — about this gathering of kids on city property, and having flares and charcoal fires going. And certainly we knew that almost no one there was legal drinking age (now 21, which seems unfair, but that's another story), and quite a few of them (or us) were drinking (or decanting) alcoholic beverages. And naturally we were aware that people in the group possessed illegal substances. But still, the reason that we ran was just that we were kids and they were cops, I think; we (three kids) believed that getting caught by cops was *always* bad, even if you maybe hadn't done whatever things it was the cops had come to catch you doing. And so, as I have said, we fled.

I was definitely in the right company to make good my escape. Lafountain was the sort of kid who had, for years, explored old dumps and landfills, shooting off his BB gun, or watching birds, or looking for old bones and bottles. So, naturally, Lafountain was the one to say, "Come on. This way. Haul ass, you deadfoot dummies."

Dori was the one who *could* haul ass, both rapidly and stylishly, far better than yours truly, especially on strange terrain. Agile as a catamount, she leaped and skidded down the slope in front of me, slaloming, grabbing little trees to balance up or change direction, all the time still giving me instructions and advice.

"Look out, it's gushy over there," she'd say. "Careful of this branch, now. Come on, there's like a little path, right here. . . ."

I followed her white shirt with very near blind faith, running into it a time or two, grabbing onto her white shoulder just before I fell. Behind us, up the slope, I vaguely heard loud-speaking going on, plus shouts and whistles, hardly sounds I'd want to be real close to, that's for sure. It seemed as if "the raid" (as what was taking place was labeled in my mind, already) was not a perfect roundup by a long shot, though. We, and others we could hear behind and to the sides of us, had broke out free and clear.

Because it was still early, yet, we made our way downtown and hung around outside this pizza joint, Gastronomico's, where we regaled some other kids (who'd chosen other forms of entertainment for the evening) with news about the party and the raid. Everybody laughed, including us, hysterically at times. How could we have known that that would be our *second* big mistake?

8
FALLOUT

My mother says before they built the dome nobody ever served a brunch in Dustin. Now, all the
brand-new restaurants in town, like Piccanteria,
Gobbo's and The Comestible Express, have brunch
on Saturdays and Sundays, both. My mother claims
that people who eat "brunch" also use the "-ish"
words, which she also can't abide.

" 'Brunch at Gobbo's? Noon-ish?' That's the way
they talk," she said on Sunday morning to Lafountain, who was at our house and bellied up to roast
beef hash with three poached eggs.

"The only difference between the thing you're
doing now and eating brunch," she said, "is that at
brunch you'd have to put some vodka in your juice
and look a little roguish, right? Big deal."

Lafountain chewed and swallowed.

"I never call it 'brunch,' I swear," he promised. "You can ask my mother. I always tell her that I'm going to go to Gabe's for *breakfast* — and *his* mother asked me. She goes: 'Breakfast? At this hour?' I go: 'Sure.' Then she goes: 'Pretty funny time for breakfast.' I go: 'Well, the food don't know it.' "

Lafountain almost always comes for Sunday breakfast, and my mother *has* invited him, for any time, although she doesn't do the cooking. Sundays, 'round about the middle of the morning (no, I'd never say 'eleven-ish'), my father and myself begin to blend our talents in order to produce a memorable meal. Actually, it's the same one, over and over. I squeeze the orange juice and flip the pancakes made from scratch — little ones, no bigger than a coaster — while he digs out his trusty can opener and makes his famous roast beef hash with fresh poached eggs. It's fair to say he does improve the hash with "secret" seasonings; he also makes a fragrant pot of coffee and unscrews the ketchup top.

"Anyway," Lafountain said. "I think they just arrested five or six of them — people who were really bombed, plus one or two that started wising off. Donald said they threw old Streeter up against a car and cuffed his wrists behind his back and everything. While Streeter told them who his father was, of course. And then they took a lot of names and issued, like, a warning, telling everyone to stay off city property except for parks at posted hours, and not to ever drink or even *hold* an open alcoholic drink in public. Or to *possess* one, underage. The next offense for anyone whose name they got would mean at least a fine and possibly imprisonment, they said.

That's what Donald told me. He was pretty frosted."

"Oh? What color? You *did* mean pretty, comma, frosted, right?" my father said. "Fudgy brown with coral pink rosettes is still *my* favorite. But how could *he* be frosted, anyway? It doesn't sound as if the cops were out of line. I mean, even two defectives like yourselves were perfectly aware you weren't meant to be there. And both of you can count to twenty-one; I'd bet our second car on it."

"But *Dad*," I said. "It *is* a Subaru. And anyway, that's not the point. I mean, I know you're right: that *technically* the party was illegal, and that people shouldn't drink and this-and-that. But — *I* don't know — to us that raid is just another part of, like, an attitude there seems to be in town. Like, everything is going great except the kids. You know? The thing is, we weren't doing anybody any harm out there, and, well, it just feels good to get away, sometimes."

"From what?" my father asked. Good guy though he is, he looked a bit incredulous.

"From everything," I said. That sounded maybe slightly overdone, and so I veered. "Like, in colonial days it used to be you could take old Tige and the muzzleloader your dad gave you on your thirteenth birthday and go for a walk in the woods. Head out to that big rock you discovered, right above a waterfall. Your secret place — you know? — and it was yours, all yours. No grown-up even knew that it was there, most likely. Only you and that Matilda Boone — "

" — who used to be a tomboy and a brat," my

37

mother said, "but who just the year before, like overnight, it seemed, had got the cutest little pair of — "

" — raccoon cubs," my father kicked back in to say. "And thank you very much for your support," he told my mother.

"But Gabe, it's true," he said, now back to me. "You modern city kids do have it rough." He poured more maple syrup on his ravaged stack of pancakes. "You have so little chance for self-expression. Your mother and I were wondering if maybe you could make a weekly tape of your opinions and ideas, that we could play a lot of times at our convenience, so that we could stay completely up-to-date — "

" — in case," my mother cut him off again, "all the people who've anonymously sent us copies of your letters to the school paper in the past — "

" — along with their suggestions for the steps that we might take to teach you better manners — "

But by that time both of them were laughing *much* too raucously for me to try to make a serious indictment of the raid.

Lafountain asked my father some Greg Norman question, and we left that other subject altogether.

Monday morning, we rejoined it, with the help of R.D. (Rollie) Morehead, Principal, and (I would bet my born-but-still-unrusted-and-undented future car on it) good Dr. Leeds.

He used the intercom, which brought his charming and informal tone of voice right into every homeroom. He sounded very much at home and, from time to time, *down* home as well. Somewhere along the line, at Chapel Hill most likely, he'd picked up just a tiny *smidgen* of a southern accent. This (I'm sure he liked to think) made him sound like very near a *pal*, to us, his younger listeners.

"This past Satiday night, I'm sorry to say" — but still he said it — "there was a party held on city property, within the limits of our town. It was attended, for the most part, by members of our school community, and so I think it's fair to say that information on the party's time and whereabouts was circulated in the classrooms and the corridors of DHS. There was, in other words, a clear connection — very near a cause-effect relationship — between this party and our school. And at the party drugs and alcohol, particularly beer, were used — consumed — by many of you here this morning, in direct violation of school policy.

"The town police have given us — the school directors and myself — the names of that small group of students who they quite regretfully arrested at the party's site — and of a much larger group who were present but not arrested. The arrested students are hereby suspended from school for ten days, under the terms of the school's stated policy concerning drugs and alcohol; they may also face prosecution and judgment in the city courts. The other students whose names we have, as well as still another sizable group of students who, we are told, chose flight to facing their responsibilities, will receive official warnings only — and in light of this *extremely* lenient, even charitable, attitude, we expect that all their names will be forthcoming. However, students who are members of a school athletic team, who have violated the school athletic code, may face still further disciplinary action on the part of their coaches.

"Should any parties of this nature reoccur, at any point in future time, we will presume the purpose of said parties to include the use of drugs and alcohol, and we — the school directors and myself — will see to it that those attending will be swiftly and severely punished."

There was a pause, then this P.S.:

"C'mon, you guys, get smart on this, okay? It's just your *lahvs* we're tryin' to save."

Uh-*huh*. We sat there stupidly or not, depending. But as the things he'd said sunk in, and then spread out into the lidded land of Dustin, there were various reactions. Moving from the larger world to the smaller, spongy one between my ears, they went as follows:

Around town, from what my parents said, the basic feeling was: Hooray! It's about time the school started Cracking Down on teenaged drug-and-drinking parties. Keep it up and sock it to 'em, Mr. er-um-*Moreland*, is it?

This was pretty much what you'd — and I'd — expect, I guess.

Inside the school, however, certain kids, though on-the-surface furious about the raid, were more relieved than anything. The school, even the cops, were acting kind of lenient, they thought. Hey, sheesh, they could have just suspended everyone. So, lots of people got a "warning," or whatever Morehead called it. Waddayaexpect

40

fahchristmasake? It wouldn't even show up on their transcripts, they were pretty sure, which meant The Great God College wouldn't mind, which meant their parents wouldn't really blow their stacks, which meant . . . well, no harm done, right? Right.

I, of course, produced my own minority opinion. So as not to disappoint my parents, I sent it in to *Dust Devils*, and here is how it read:

To the editor:

So now we have the latest from the ruling *troika* of fair Dustin's only downtown *gulag* — a.k.a. this high school. Did you hear what I heard?

1. A daffynition, from the lips of spokesman Mr. Morehead:
   school-related activity (*n.*) a. Anything that's talked about in school, by students, that later they are active in. Question: What does this make s–x, one wonders?

2. A suggestion, also as per Mr. M.:
   Anyone who plays a part in any school-related activity (see daffynition, above) which the School (that's its Directors) disapproves of, shall run and tell the School about the part they played, just in case It hasn't heard already.

3. Corollary to above suggestion:
   Telling on your friends who played such parts, or even people you don't know, vill help der School to do a better chob.

4. Final ominous warning (source, the same):
   From now on, parties of "this nature" are *verboten*, got it? Their purpose is "presumed," you see.

Achtung! Dos Vidanya (sp?)!
                    Gabriel Podesta, Junior Class

9
GUILTY PARTY

I don't know how long the "school athletic code" has been around. It strikes me as an eighties kind of thing. According to its terms, if you're sufficiently endowed with skillful, silky moves, and strength, and swiftness — and with fire in your belly, I presume — to represent the school in sports, you get to sign a pledge.

(English subtitle: "He's jealous.")

Dori *hated* signing it. By doing so, she promised not to use tobacco, alcohol or drugs. And if she did, she'd take whatever punishment her coach and the athletic council said was fair, up to and including mutilation (of her pride).

"Yuck. It made me feel *unclean*," she said to me the day she did it. "I told Coach Brautigan. I told her that it wasn't any ath-uh-letic honor code that

43

made *me* train. You can guess what *she* said."

" 'Is-so, is-so, is-so, is-so'?" I said. We were sitting side by side before the tube; the tube was in the den in my house. It was Sunday. I was eating Champ's potato chips, which went with Giants football games.

"No, you moron," Dori said. She grabbed a handful of my chips; they're made with peanut oil, so Dori says they aren't junk food. "She said that be that as it may, *now* if I saw someone on the team break training, I would know I had a teammate who I couldn't count on, and I'd *want* to turn her in. Is that a crock, or what?"

"Well, I don't know," I said. Teasing Dori's irresistible, sometimes. "It'd probably depend on what *position* she played, and whether she's starting and you're not, and — "

Dori flung herself toward me on the couch, grabbed me by the shoulders and began to shake me. I just relaxed and played along. I'd asked for it. Besides, it didn't feel that bad, and anyway, I'd get her back. I always do. It's part of the relationship.

"Gabe Podesta," she was yelling, "you're just trying to make me mad." She stopped shaking me. "Just look at your hair," she said. She licked her palms and smoothed it back in place, as if I were a four-year-old.

"Coercion's what it is," she said. "If you don't sign that pledge you can't play *jacks* for Dustin High. I believe in working out, in keeping training, you know that. I don't use that junk. Look," — she pulled her shirt up, pinched the skin that covered her flat belly — "there ain't no flab on me. But that's

44

because I *choose* . . . hey, cut it out. Hey, stop that, Gabe, you little monster! I'm going to call your *mother* if you. . . ."

Of course I'd grabbed her for a flab test of my own, flinging her across my knees so I could do some careful research on her fanny.

"Vait," I said, trying to hold her wrists together so's to keep her guarding hands away, "I get der calipers and den ve see if dis is bottom round or vot. . . ." The combination of some stiff and tight new jeans and her well-muscled rump was making my job difficult. But I persevered. A hard worker is a happy worker, as my father often says.

"Okay, you asked for it." Her voice was muffled by the sofa cushion, but the mission of her vengeful hand seemed all too clear. I quickly dumped her off my lap and down onto the rug.

"You fink," she said. "You'd be perfect for the Dustin ath-uh-letic honor code. You'd love to turn a teammate in. I'd like to turn *you* in — for sexual harrassment. I'm going to tell your mother what you do to me, behind her back."

"*Do* to you?" I said. I bounced my eyes between the Giants (on the Eagle 24) and Dori (sitting at my feet). "All I was, was checking your . . . veracity. Checking out your worthiness to die for dear old Dustin. Besides — what you were saying — colleges have honor systems, too, you know. Some colleges."

"Yeah," she said. "But they're completely different. What they're about is cheating, like on schoolwork. I can see that cheating on the *purpose* of the place, the whole damn institution, that would be

45

completely unacceptable. And anyway, if students at a college didn't want an honor system, they could just get rid of it, I bet. We don't have that option."

"But still, you signed the thing," I said. Giants on the Eagle 8.

"Because I want to *play*," she said. "I didn't have a *choice*. How many times must I explain that to you, *mush-head*? Believe me, this girl's chest swells not with pride."

"Well," I started, leaning forward, peering at that part of her anatomy. It was covered by a shirt and sweatshirt, naturally. "Perhaps I should look into that. If it isn't pride it must be . . ." Dori rose up to her knees and spread her hand out on my face, and shoved. I slumped back on the couch; my eyes made contact with the silver screen. ". . . Mark Bavaro, touchdown!" I concluded.

That was pretty near two months ago. Wednesday, after dinner, she called up and asked if I'd come over to her house. She didn't joke around at all. She said that she had something that she had to tell me, "Now." I said I'd be right over.

Dori and her father lived in a little house set in a neighborhood of little houses. It was about the only part of town where parents bought *themselves* used cars.

Mr. Fabb worked at the Dustin library; he and Dori's mother got divorced when we were in the seventh grade. I remember, to my everlasting squirm, that I avoided Dori for a while right after everybody'd heard about her parents splitting up. The thing was this: Divorce, one parent moving out of town, away, that scared me. It was *too* mysterious for me, back then: why it happened, how it worked.

Dori met me at the door. She looked as if she'd run a marathon, completely whipped.

"Poppy's real upset," she said, in just above a whisper. "I didn't want to leave him, but I had to talk to you. I'm off the soccer team. It's total garbage, Gabe — the worst. What I'd like to do is throw a fit, but with him the way he is, I've got to try and not act too emotional, okay?"

I nodded, feeling sort of clang-y in my head; I followed her into the kitchen.

Llewellyn Fabb is No Fun at the best of times. Not that he is cruel, cantankerous or condescending (3 C's we teens, historically, have been exposed to). What he is, is solemn, super-solemn. Appearance-wise, he is a stocky guy with Dori's curly hair and a neatly trimmed brown beard, the kind that's like a strip around a person's chin and doesn't have a mustache to go with it. He always looks a little stunned. Two-three hundred years ago, guys with looks like his smoked long clay pipes and traded rum for beaver pelts, but never at too good a profit. Nowadays, they're usually mechanics at a really big garage, the kind who've usually got their heads inside a car and never chat with customers. In fact, he owns a '67 Buick Skylark, and he works on it a lot.

If he isn't working on his car, Mr. Fabb is usually sitting at the kitchen table with a mug of tea and an open book. He leaves the living room for Dori and myself. Many times, when I come in, though, he doesn't appear to be reading. He'll just be sitting there, looking either out the window at the yard, or possibly just off in space. He's so completely different from my father.

I always smile and act real friendly toward the guy. I wish that I could forge some *bond* between us, man to man, so I could start to love him. He's Dori's father, after all. That I could ever call him "Llew" is pretty inconceivable, right now.

"Hi, Mr. Fabb," is what I said, as usual, that night. I decided to omit the smile.

"Good evening, Gabe," he said. He didn't look at me, but in between us, somewhere. "Would you like a cup of tea? Or seltzer? Or some orange juice?"

I looked at Dori. Would I?

"I'll get some seltzer for us, Pop," she said. "Gabe's come because I asked him. He's got to hear what happened. Possibly he'll have some thoughts. I'll take him to the living room. Join us if you want to."

That's the way she talked to him. As if she were an adult, too. *The* adult, maybe.

He nodded. I just took the glass that Dori handed me and followed her again, although I threw a smile at Mr. Fabb as I went out. He didn't see it. He was back into his staring mode — out or off, whichever.

"This is the pits," said Dori, quietly, when we had settled in our places. She was on the couch, her legs tucked under her; I sat on the floor, leaning back against the chair that looked to me as if it might have been her father's, in the days before he'd settled in the kitchen.

Here's the story that she told me, minus frills.

That afternoon, she'd gone to soccer practice, naturally. But DeDe Brautigan, the coach, had made the squad sit down, instead of starting drills, the way she always did. There was this little grandstand, right there by the middle of the field.

She said they "had to have a little talk about the Stanchion Party." First of all, who'd been there? ("She thought she was so cool, the way she knew the name of it," said Dori.)

After a little nervous silence, this one girl, Amy Beliveau, had said she guessed *she* had; the cops had taken down her name, she thought. But, she said, she hadn't broken training, she'd just been there with some friends, like hanging out. She swore it.

Coach Brautigan then said that Amy'd made a bad mistake by going to the party, but that based on information she had gotten in the past two days, she believed her when she said she hadn't broken training, or the code. She said that Amy Beliveau would run five extra laps right after practice, please. And she hoped she'd learned a lesson.

Then she asked if anybody else had anything to say. No one seemed to, this time; people looked at one another, but nobody spoke.

The coach then sighed this real big sigh and said, "Okay, let's have the following out here, and facing toward this sideline." She named eight names, including "Fabb." Dori'd thought that maybe they were going to do some drill, a new one.

Not so, not even close. "First of all," Ms. Brautigan began, "we have the case of Bemis, Ward, Ragazzo, Jordan, Miksch, and Feltenstein."

"That's just the way she said it," Dori said to me. " '*The case of*.' You could tell that she was *furious*."

She knew, the coach went on to say, that these

six girls were *also* at the party. Their names had not been taken by the town police, nor had they turned *themselves* in, as the principal had asked. They had run away; they thought that they'd escaped responsibility. Was that correct?

The six looked down and then at one another. Then they started nodding, all of them.

But, Ms. Brautigan went on, they hadn't broken training — was that right? Like Beliveau, they'd just been "hanging out."

This time the nods came instantly, with little smiles.

The coach did not return the smiles. These girls would run *ten* extra laps, right after practice, she declared, the extra five for not admitting they were there when they'd been told to. She paused and then said, no, they'd better run *fifteen*, another five for not obeying the police, for running off to start with.

That brought her, finally, to "Fabb and Johnson." "Here we have the prime offenders," she began. "Take a *good* look at them, girls. . . ."

They, she said, were also at the party and they also had run off and not admitted they were there. But they — "these two" — had *also* broken training, and the school athletic code. Both of them had drunk some beer, and Johnson had smoked cigarettes, as well. But now, she said, "their chickens have come home to roost."

"Can you imagine that?" Dori said to me. "Her telling *me* my 'chickens had come home to roost'? Like hell they had."

And so, Coach Brautigan continued, the two of them were off the team, as of that moment, but as punishment for violating the school athletic code, they would report to practice every day and run around the field as long as practice lasted.

Rachel Johnson, Dori said, began to cry at once. She didn't even try to speak, she only stood there, crying.

"I," said Dori Fabb to me, "was also speechless — for a different reason, though. You've heard that phrase 'struck dumb'? I swear I was struck dumb, for possibly two minutes, there."

Meanwhile, DeDe Brautigan just kept on talking, Dori said. But now she shifted gears and sounded sorrowful and martyred, tried to, anyway. "Miz Nice Guy," Dori said. "Ho-ho."

She started with a proud-to-be-from-Dustin rap: what kind of town this was, the kind of reputation that it had, the kind of people living here. They were, the great majority (she said) the kind of people you could count on, who would keep their word and always do their best — team players, good competitors, and winners. She was sorry, she went on to say, that Fabb and Johnson weren't worthy of the trust that all "the rest of us" had placed in them. That cans of beer and cigarettes had meant more to them than their teammates' respect, and their words of honor. She wasn't saying they were "bad," just "weak" (she guessed); possibly, they'd been talked into it by other people, maybe out-of-towners — though that wasn't an excuse. Now, regrettably, as she had said, their chickens had come home to roost and they must pay for their mistakes. She told the squad that while some vengeful thoughts on their part would be . . . "well, only human," that they should strive to rise above those feelings and feel sorry for the two. *She* had set their punishment, with the approval of the School Athletic Council. Of course she'd like to think that that would be the end of it. Except for some small mention on their transcripts, she imagined.

" 'And now,' she said," said Dori, " 'we can finally start our practice.' Can you imagine that? *I'd* been accused and tried and sentenced by this *person*, and she thought that that was it, and they could just start *practice*?" She made a snarling sound, curling up her lip.

"By then I had my voice back, so I yelled 'Hold on!' " she said. "Like, really yelled it. Brautigan just looked at me and said, 'If I were you, I'd keep my mouth shut, Dori. You're only going to make it worse. I have my facts from witnesses, you know.' "

"God," I said. "So what did you say?"

"I said 'The hell you do,' " said Dori. "And then I said I wanted everyone to hear my side of it. And that part of what they'd heard was totally untrue."

"First, I said that, yes, I had been at the party, but that I hadn't spoken up because I happened to believe it wasn't any business of the school's or of the coach's where I went on weekends. I said I didn't drink that night — not beer or any other alcoholic drink — or smoke tobacco or use any drug. And I said anyone who said I did was lying. And then," said Dori, and she started crying, "I started crying."

"God," I said again, "how awful."

I crawled the two steps to the couch and grabbed her knee. That may not be a recognized technique for giving consolation to a friend, but it was all I could come up with at the time, given my belief that Dori's crying might well bring her father to the scene.

"What did Brautigan do then?" I asked.

"She said, again, that she was sorry," Dori said. She sniffed and blew her nose. "But she had witnesses who'd seen me 'totally intoxicated' — back in town, I bet, when we were eating pizza, reeking of the beer you got all over us. And furthermore, she felt I had 'an attitude.' She reminded me that I had 'made a fuss' about the code before the season even started, and that my attitude toward her and toward the school's authority was 'immature and unacceptable.' She suggested that I take a long hard look and see what kind of *person* I was turning into."

"*I'd like to kill that woman.*"

I jumped about a foot and let go of Dori's knee. Mr. Fabb was standing in the doorway from the kitchen, and I hadn't heard him coming.

"I'm calling up my lawyer in the morning," he went on to say. He was gripping both sides of the doorjamb, tightly, just about at shoulder height. He looked as if he was keeping himself from rushing into the room and doing God knows what.

"Mr. Jerry Koch," he said, now looking straight at me. "She isn't going to get away with this. I won't have Dori's reputation ruined by this *bitch*."

I nodded rapidly, wanting him to see how much the two of us agreed on that. Meanwhile, I was thinking: "lawyer," "ruined reputation." Doink.

Dori's mother hadn't gotten custody; there had to be a reason. Two years before, when I had started feeling things for Dori — not going out with her, just feeling things — I'd asked my mother: Why, why, why? What happened? What's the story?

"I've heard she played around," she'd told me, finally. "That was what 'they' said, back then — the ones who always seem to know that kind of stuff. I have no reason to think that, myself; nothing's ever simple, cut and dried. I never got to know her. She was very pretty and I always thought I'd like her and I ought to call her up sometime. I never did, and now she's moved to Oregon, or so I've heard. If I sound a little mad, I am. At me, and them, and how things work, sometimes. And now you know as much as I do and I hope you're satisfied."

I wasn't but I said I was. What else could I say? Sometimes, I ask too many questions.

Dori only talked to me about her mother once. She said, "I know she loved me, but she left. I don't know why. Talking makes it worse; you start to speculate. I don't like to do that. I just want to love her and I do. That's all. She wasn't anything the way they said she was; I know that much." I figured that her father told her that he didn't know the reason that her mother'd left.

"This goddam town . . ." Llewellyn Fabb was saying softly in the doorway, almost to himself.

10
DO'S AND DON'T'S, PART TWO

"Don't mind *them*."

Of course I first heard that one from my mother. Mothers are the queens of do's and don't's, the civilizing process. You tend to thank them for it, later on. Though maybe not out loud. No one likes to see a mother looking smug.

"Gabriel's a *girl's* name." Ronnie Gervais chanted that at kindergarten recess, and I told my mom. Fifty little copycats joined in with him, or maybe it was four. And I was miserable.

"Don't mind *them*," she said.

It helped — a little. What really helped was finding out, next day in school, that Rotten Ronnie'd found another target for his gibes.

She told me those three words at other times, as

well, during other grade school crises. Like, after Nora Hoyt observed, and mentioned to my third grade class (in, like, a piercing scream) that I was wearing light pink underwear. My briefs had gotten washed with Dad's new flannel nightshirt.

In time, I noticed there were people who my mother minded, too. My mother, the psychologist. Same thing with my father, who was just the coolest guy I knew.

She minded being called a murderess, outside her clinic. *He* minded when some golfers on the tour told him that Ronald Reagan would be among the top five finishers as greatest American President "in the judgment of historians."

"Historians!" he squawked. "These are guys who think Grover Cleveland is an old-time pitcher in the Baseball Hall of Fame. That Benjamin Harrison was 'this good ole boy from Arkansas that used to play the tour.' "

We mind. It's a part of the human condition (as I've been known to say, when I'm explaining some small person-truth to my dear friend, Lafountain). And most of all we mind when we are hit in parts of us we value. Our character and honor, just for instance.

Here is what got sprayed on Dori's locker, early on the next school day. In black, and white, and Day-Glo orange paint.

"Traitor," "Bitch" and "Loser-Boozer."

11
A
REAL
MISUNDERSTANDING

Dori didn't run her laps around the soccer field that day. Rachel Johnson did, I understand, but Dori didn't. She didn't go to any classes after the first period, either. One look at all that painted garbage on her locker, and she marched straight to the Office and reported it. And asked for an appointment with the principal.

"I was going to do this anyway, but after school," she snapped in my direction. Not *at* me, in my direction. "Now it just won't wait."

Naturally, the secretaries said that Morehead was booked solid for the day. And that furthermore — worst luck — he'd be leaving for some Perfect Pleasant Principal's Convention, first thing in the morning. Far away, in either Rio de Janeiro or . . .

Papeete, was it? They could look it up. It wasn't any Hackensack, they knew that much.

Dori smiled her sweetest smile and told them not to bother. And she added that she guessed she'd just sit "there" — she pointed to a chair outside of Morehead's door — each day and starting then, until the principal returned and found the time to see her.

Half an hour later — all of this hearsay, but believe it — a secretary came and said, "Well, *you're* the lucky one." Mr. Morehead had a cancellation and would "squeeze her in."

Dori thinks she knows how come she got so "lucky." She believes that Morehead, hearing she was camped outside his door, called up Leeds, T. Hank, or Teagle for advice. And that way he found out that Mr. Jerry Koch had got in touch with Mr. Jamison, attorney for the school, and said he'd bet him possibly a thousand bucks that he could prove that Dori Fabb was straight as Sister Rita's ruler, back in Mater Cristi Elementary. And that the stuff that had gone down would make a dandy story when he told it, Jerry (maybe) said, emphasizing "when he told it." Besides being an attorney, Mr. Koch was the host of a very popular radio call-in show that aired throughout the region, Thursday mornings.

In any case, when she was seated there in Morehead's office, admiring his very pale blue shirt and rep silk tie, Dori told him, number one, that she was innocent of any violation of the school athletic code. So, number two: She, her father and their lawyer planned to sue the school and its directors, Ms. Coach of Soccer Brautigan, the School Athletic

58

Council, and ". . . er, sorry, sir, *yourself* . . ." for damages.

"I've been humiliated and defamed," she told the principal. "My present reputation and my future plans have both been jeopardized by accusations that are false and irresponsible."

Dori said he started making "but-but" sounds, while trying to still look suave and genial, a little bit above it all.

"*However*," Dori said. And she went on to say that maybe they would reconsider (her lawyer and her father and herself), if he would do the following: Call the School Athletic Council to convene at once; let her be faced with her accusers, Coach's "witnesses" (so-called); then let *her* produce *her* witnesses, people like Lafountain and myself who'd spent all Stanchion Party evening in her company. And who could tell the Council just exactly why she *smelled* of Miller High Life, although she hadn't sampled any.

Mr. Morehead nodded thoughtfully and said, "Mmm-hmm." Then he suggested that she resume her regularly scheduled program while he considered her "request."

Dori said, "With all respect, it isn't really a 'request'. . . ." She also said there wasn't any point in walking through a normal day — that she was too upset to learn.

Morehead said "but-but" it might be *days* before the Council members — "all real busy folks" — could find the time. . . .

Dori rose and said that she would wait outside, and see. If the Council couldn't find the time that day, she said, she guessed they'd have to find it later in the month, answering some court's subpoena.

What she thinks happened next is this: As soon as she got out of there, Morehead left his office by the other door. And raced down to a conference with Dr. Leeds. (Did I mention he had moved his office to inside the school, and now saw patients there?) Dori liked imagining some close-to-naked matron in a little gown, sitting on a chilly, paper-covered table waiting for the doc to reappear, while Roland David Morehead made completely sure that he could blame whatever he was going to do on someone higher up.

Dori thinks that Morehead *then* went further down the hall to Ruggiero ("Ratsy") Rizzo's office. Rizzo is our school's AD, as well as its head football coach; he was a great, great All-American at Pitt, a nose guard, I believe. Rizzo doubtless called in Brautigan and then whichever kids it was that she said fingered Dori in the first place.

About a quarter box of tissues later, Dori reckoned, Morehead (also) knew the truth: No one ever saw Dorinda drinking any beer on Saturday, although (sniff-sniff) she certainly had *smelled* of it, and acted "like, completely waffled."

Dori bet that Brautigan then screamed at her false witnesses, who doubtless left the office still in tears, and that then Coach Rizzo screamed at *her*. Morehead was a crooner, not a screamer, so Dori bet when his turn came, he walked all over Rizzo in that charming way of his, probably suggesting that this incident just *proved* what he'd been saying, that the whole athletic staff was "ovuhpaid."

He also must have sat there while Coach Brautigan

wrote out, and let him check the spelling on, and signed, a notice he could post which said Dorinda Fabb was innocent of any violation of the school athletic code.

Whether all that's just exactly right or not, we'll never know. But this much is plain fact. At a quarter after two that afternoon, Mr. Morehead ambled out his office door, his face all wreathed in smiles. And in his hand he held a notice like the one described above.

"Well, young lady," he began. He sat down in the chair beside Dorinda and he positively *beamed*. "I've done my own investigation of your case, and you are right. There's been a real *misunderstanding* here. Coach Brautigan is just delighted that it's all cleared up, and you . . . your slate's been wahped completely clean!" He showed the notice to her.

"I'll just be posting this." He gave her his clean hand to shake. "I'm glad you came to me. That's just exactly what I'm heah for."

Dori swore he had a clean *white* shirt on, and a different tie.

When she called me up that night and told me this whole story, I asked her what about the soccer team. Did she want to keep on playing? Dori said she didn't know; she thought she'd go to Brautigan, next day, and sort of test the waters.

"After all," she said to me. "I guess she did admit that she was wrong."

Ho-ho-ho, as it turned out. The next day was another day, for sure. Dori found the coach in the equipment room right after lunch. And her answer to Dorinda's overture started with a huge, derisive snort. Dori hadn't gotten drunk on beer perhaps, said Brautigan, but still there was the matter of her "attitude."

"You're never going to play for me as long as I'm at Dustin High," this lady told Dorinda. And then she looked this way and that, behind her, making double sure that this was private, just between the two of them.

Then she pointed right at Dori's breastbone and unloaded this: "You got me in a whole shitload of trouble, you damn whiny little bitch!"

12
DEAR GOVERNOR (1)

Dear Governor,

I saw an article somewhere which said that you believe that certain values should be *taught* in public schools. That's "taught," instead of just discussed, in context, in a lot of different classes, the way it happens, or *should* happen, now.

That makes me want to ask some questions:

1. Who would be the one to make the list of *which*, exactly?
2. And how they would be taught?
3. By whom?

And hasn't this been tried before, in Germany, Iran, and elsewhere?

> Respectfully and sincerely,
> Gabriel Podesta, Junior Class

13
VALUES I

"Because we don't have any textbook for our values classes," Varney said, "it's been decided that we'd start — I and all the other social studies teachers — by reading . . . well, this *essay*, here. Think of it as, like, a kind of *backboard*, maybe — something all of you can bounce your own ideas and comments and reactions off of. I haven't had the chance to read it, myself, but as I guess you've guessed, it's on the topic 'Fairness.' "

I put my hand up, instantly.

"Hey, look at that," said Varney. "Is this the way to go, or what? I haven't even started yet, and here's the first reaction." Laughter. "Gabe?"

"Question, not reaction, Mr. Poole. Just curious," I said. "Who wrote this thing you're going to read? Aristotle? Teilhard de Chardin? Art Buchwald?"

Color me suspicious, I don't mind. How about a nice, bright mauve?

"Beats me," said Varney. "Probably some prof, somewhere. High-priced college profs *cause* all the classroom innovation, nowadays. Handsome guys like me are just the *symptoms* of what's happening. All I know is Mr. Matthews passed them out to us in our department meeting just before first hour, and he didn't say who wrote them. Not that I remember, anyway. Okay?"

I nodded, narrowing my eyes for the effect.

"And so away we go," said Varney, looking at the typescript in his hand.

" 'Long before the phoney freedom fetishists, the pastors of *permitio*, began to preach and promulgate their. . . .' "

Oh, sure. I looked across the room and caught Lafountain's eye. I touched my earlobe, then pretended to caress some something hanging down from it.

Lafountain looked the way a setter dog does, when he sees you put your boots on. He lip-synched silently a certain single syllable.

Correct, correct, oh, fountain of great truths. No "high-priced college prof" had written this. Unless we missed our guesses, *this* was from a source just down the stairs one flight, and to the right a ways. From Dustin's Pat Buchanan write-alike, Herr School Direktor Leeds!

Varney hadn't noticed our exchange, of course. Head down, tripping over words from time to time, he kept on with his reading.

Once Leeds had finished off the Justice Brennan-Doctor Spock enthusiasts, he sort of settled down and focused on the topic: Fairness. He started by reminding us, his gentle hearers, that all of us had ancestors ("no doubt") who first came to America in order to escape its opposite — *Un*fairness — in the country of their origin. Religious persecution, social inequality, ersatz criminality et cetera were what propelled our great granddaddies toward these shores. (At that point I decided not to check and see how any of the black kids in the class were taking all of this; frankly, it was too embarrassing.)

Next, he picked up on the causes of our Revolution. Among the many good examples of that old King George the Third's unfairness, he dealt both long and faithfully with how he'd taxed the colonists who had no voice at all in England's Parliament. By contrast, he continued, we could take the U.S. Constitution, with all its guarantees that everyone would get the same fair treatment from the government. ("Though recently," he couldn't help but add, "perhaps we've overdone it to the point of being fairer to the creeps and criminals that prowl the streets than to their hapless victims.")

But over and above all that, Leeds (and Varney Poole) went on to say, there is this specially — *peculiarly* — American respect for fairness. It's typified (they said) by certain phrases that are heard throughout the land, from north to south and east to west. We hear "Play fair" and "That ain't fair"; "He won it fair and square." Good hits in baseball are "fair" balls. From our earliest childhood we are taught to play within the rules, to earn advantages by skill and by hard work, and to scorn deceit and trickery — taking an "unfair" advantage of another person.

When Varney finished reading all of that and more, lots of people clapped, including me. Face it, I can be as fair as anyone. And so, I didn't overdo it.

"Now, I ask you," Varney said. "What do you think, guys? Is fairness *hot*, or what? Is it a *Now* commodity? Yes — Laura?"

"It all depends on what you want to talk about," said Laura Stanton. "I know that everybody's going to mock me, but . . . when you look at what we've done to the Native Americans. . . ."

Of course a lot of classmates moaned, in chorus. Laura drags her favorite people into everything; you'd think she'd grown up planting maize and masticating beaver skins. No matter what the topic is, she's apt to find some way to link it to the crummy deal the Indians have always gotten. The fact that she's completely right just makes it all the more annoying. Our country's as fair as they come, yet we *can* be better still.

But Varney waved her off, as usual.

I decided I'd be teacher's friend, regardless, and so when he then asked if we could give him some examples of old Fairness in America today, I pitched right in. My dad had told me that pro golfers on the tour would actually call penalty strokes against themselves, if their ball moved in the rough before they hit it, or they accidentally grounded a club in a sand trap. Nobody else even *sees* these things happen, mind you, and they call it anyway.

"That's really being fair," I said, "when you put the interests of the *game*, and of the other *players*, ahead of your own personal lust for money and endorsements and all that."

"I think that's being *stupid*," Arby Fremont said. "How would they know how many other people *aren't* doing that? They could be giving themselves a right royal screwing."

"Yeah," I said, "but still — you got to do it your way, don't you? Who wants to spend their lifetime just trying to keep from getting screwed?"

People laughed, and someone in the back said, "Don't worry. The women of America will see to that in your case, Gabe."

"Gabriel — my friend," said Arby, sounding weary, way above it all. "That's exactly what you *have* to do. Grow up. Be realistic. We're in the eighties, now. Let me give you an example: getting into college. Suppose I see my SAT's are low, compared to yours. Well, then, I'm going to go and take a special course; my dad'll spring for that, with pleasure. Now, you can say that that's not fair to all the kids who can't afford the course — or maybe they don't even have one where they live. It also maybe means that *you* are going to have to take the course as well, to try to stay ahead of me. But don't you see? That isn't anything but life. That's competition, man."

"Same thing with business," Deano Dobbins said. "When my old man is out there on the lot, he's trying to sell a car — at max. If you're dumb enough to give him what the sticker says, that's *your* problem."

"Of course the rules are understood," said Varney. "And it cuts both ways. When I'm trading in my clunker, I'm not about to tell your dad that its transmission's shot." And he and Deano laughed, and Deano said, "Hell, no."

"Or with my mom," said Tammi Watrous. "She's art director down at Chatham Barnes? She isn't going to say some client's product's bad for you, even if she knows it is. She's doing *advertising*. Her job is to *sell* whatever it may be, not pass judgment on it. And hey, get this. She told me they have ways, like using certain colors, that'll make you *want* to buy the thing. Like with cigarettes — you want a lot of *white* on the package, right? That makes the buyer think they're really clean and all, you know? No germs or anything like that."

"What the consumer has to do is use his head," said Varney. "Read the label and all that. The information's there, all right, if you can understand it. That's where the fairness enters in. So, possibly the print's a little fine. . . ." He did a comic squint, pretending he was looking at a package; almost everybody laughed.

"They always say they're going to make the tax laws fair," Lafountain said, "but everybody knows there's ways to get around them. . . ."

"It's all like some big *game*," said Arby. "The smartest players get to make and keep the biggest pile of tokens, right? Everybody knows it doesn't have a thing to do with fairness — it's a game. They try to catch the cheaters, but they only get the dumb ones. The moral of the story is: Get smart."

"Sad but true," said Varney. "You don't find a lot of dumb guys sitting up near midfield at the

Super Bowl. Or lying on the beach at Acapulco. But still. There are some situations where you look for total fairness, right? Let's see if we can name a few of them."

"You mean, like parents with their kids?" said Arby. "Seems to me that'd be one. They oughtn't to play favorites."

"*Good*," said Varney. "Any others?"

"Well, judges should be fair," Lafountain said. "And juries."

"And if you're playing cards, or tennis," someone else threw in, "you shouldn't cheat, or pretty soon nobody'll play with you."

"Cops should *usually* be fair," said Deano. "Unless they *know* they've got the guy that did it. And *teachers*. Teachers *really* should be fair. I mean, if teachers aren't fair, a school will really be screwed up."

Varney smiled and did a real deep bow, and people laughed and clapped. I hadn't looked at Dori all that class, but somehow I could sense she wasn't doing either.

14
PHYS ED

"Living with my father, nowadays," said Dori, "is driving me insane."

She was with me in my basement, in what my mother called The Gym, running on my father's treadmill. That made her talk in bursts, a bunch of words stuck in between the necessary breathing.

"It's just that — little extra something — you don't need," she added. "Like it'd be if, say — the house was burning down — and running to get out — you stubbed your toe."

She looked down at the bar in front of her, to see how far she'd gone. My father's treadmill has this LCD on it that gives you facts like that about your workout. How far you've gone while getting no-where. The whole deal's sort of like the SAT's.

I was sitting on my father's rower, watching her.

But rowing, too — upstream, of course; you always go upstream. I think that's required by the Protestant ethic; using a rowing machine seems very Protestant to me. Watching Dori would appeal to all religions, though certain Catholics might be tempted to engage in mortal sin, watching Dori run. Sometimes I turn on the little TV we have down there, when I'm rowing or riding the exercise bike, but TV can't compete with Dori in the flesh. Or in the flesh *and* silver high tech fabric, to be more precise. I don't know if it was technically a swimsuit or a leotard she had on; in either case it was a very, very high-cut tank-suit-looking-deal that didn't offer any major wind resistance, or restrict her range of motion in the slightest.

"What's he doing different?" I inquired, cautiously. I never run down other people's parents, even when the other people start in doing that, themselves. People dump on their own parents constantly, but let some other unrelated voice join in, and one-time dumper presto-changeos into lioness with cubs.

"Nothing all that different," she replied. "Just more so — He's really down on Brautigan of course — He'd like to make her reinstate me — I *told* him that I'd never play for her, he doesn't care — He just wants to *hurt* her — Really bad."

"Yeah, I guess," I said, agreeably. I raised the level of resistance on each "oar" — increased the Mississippi's current, so to speak. I may be a lousy dancer, but that doesn't mean I don't have plans to build this bod of mine into a . . . into a kind of *masterpiece*. You know, the kind a girl like Dori Fabb could hardly keep her little patties offa.

"He thinks her attitude — is just a *symptom* — hey, you like that one? — a symptom of the changes that he thinks — have taken place in Dustin since the dome," said Dori. "People getting weird — thinking if they crack down on the kids — everything will be, like, hunky-dory."

"Well," I said, "some parents *are* real spooked by alcohol and drugs. It's all the Nancy Reagan stuff, all over the TV. What it does is justify their getting really militant. Saying we can't handle freedom, we abuse it."

"So everybody suffers for — the stuff some kids are doing," Dori said. "And the *causes* of the problem — never get addressed at all — Why kids turn into drunks and druggies — Why anybody does."

"I know," I said. I stopped my rowing. I'd gotten up to Memphis, from New Orleans. Incredible athleticism. Now I thought I'd like to ride the bike, let D be dazzled by my swirling thighs. I'd ride the bike to Terre Haute, perhaps. I like the sound of Terre Haute. High ground.

"You through with that?" asked Dori, pointing at the rower.

"Yeah," I said. I posed for her: elbows bent, both fists in the air, brawn just popping out all over. "I thought I'd do the bike a while." I gestured, casually. "Probably the seat's still warm, though."

"Oh, thrills," she said. She made her retching sound and pushed a button on the treadmill, made it stop. She checked the information on the dials.

"Who needs crummy soccer, anyway?" she said. "I bet I'll stay in better shape just working out with you. Plus, this way I can get some arm and shoulder strength. Build my upper body up." She looked down at her breasts and smiled, then jumped into a ninja stance before I could react.

"Hi-YAH!" She faked an open-handed chop at me.

"I'll teach you fail-ness, Doctah Reeds," she said.

I had to smile, myself. Dori — she was such a package. Lots of times, I'd merely take one glance at her and then break out into a huge delighted grin. I guess I loved the way she was, it's just that simple. We weren't all that much the same, although we did agree on major things, like faithfulness and funny. She was much more independent, moodier and more impulsive; she worried more than I did, and she also did seem older, sometimes, too.

I figured this was due to our extremely different childhoods. In my house, everything was cool and kind of . . . light, while Dori's twig was bent in turmoil and uncertainty, her father's special brand of gloom. I felt bad about that happening to her, but still I wouldn't want to change how she'd turned out, her basic Dori-ness. Change *anything* and she'd be different, someone else. If you're smart, you don't go messing with a masterpiece. You don't say, "Hey, I think I'd like that better in a green, Picasso."

This time, Dori smiled right back at me and walked across the room and kissed me on the lips. I hadn't gotten on the bike, yet. I put my arms around her sweaty back (that had a little spandex criss-cross on it), and felt her overheated front against my heart et cetera. I ran my hands straight down her back, onto and around her butt. She'd

74

been completely right: no flab. Just total and transcendent Fabb.

I knew what Dori looked like, underneath her suit. I'd known since early in the summer, just this year — the first week in July, it was. We'd gone swimming at a neighbor's house and come back home to change. My parents weren't there. Dori'd gone into the bathroom off the hall, and I into my room — as usual, so far. But moments later, came a knock-knock on my door.

"Hey, Gabe," said Dori softly, through the door. "I've got a proposition for you. How about a little game of general practitioner? That's grown-up Doctor, just in case you didn't know. We could do it taking turns and swear to *only* look, all right? No touching or et ceteras."

I'm sure I froze and probably I held my breath as well. The subject had come up before, but kiddingly. Half-kiddingly. "What difference would it make. . . ?", that kind of thing. But now — this was a serious suggestion. Gulp. I'd just pulled off my trunks. I looked into the mirror on my closet door and was not impressed or reassured at all. But still.

"I guess . . ." I said, feeling sort of eight years old.

"Here's the way we'll do it, then," said Dori. She clearly had the whole thing planned, down to the last detail. "I'll look first, because it's my idea. You strip and tell me when, and then you *close your eyes*, and I'll come in and take my look. You have to keep your eyes closed, though. That way, you don't have to see me looking — which'd be embarrassing for both of us. Then, when I'm all done — I'm only going to walk around you once — I'll go back to the bathroom. Then it'll be your turn. I'll say 'Ready,' and I'll close my eyes, and you can come and look. And when you're done, you come back here, and both of us get dressed and . . . well, that's that. We'll both have satisfied" — she laughed — "our natural curiosities. And, I don't know — there'll be a sort of . . . dumb thing gotten over with, gone bye-bye. The 'don't look' dopiness, I mean."

"Well . . . okay, I guess," I said again. "I'm sort of . . . I don't know. I hope you don't expect . . . *you* know." I wasn't thrilled with the idea. Or maybe I *was* thrilled — that and very scared, as well. Talking and touching were different than just *standing* there. I mean, we'd learned a lot about each other's bodies, and we knew how much we loved each other, but this seemed sort of unromantic. All the other stuff we'd done had been in *context*, you might say. And in the semidark.

"We don't have to," Dori said. "I'm not trying to *start* anything, you know. At all. More the opposite, if anything. But maybe it's too radical an idea. What I thought was just it would be . . . nice. I'd hate it if I . . . well, got mangled in a train wreck . . . *you* know. I've got no plans or expectations, Gabe. It was just a thing I thought of. Really, we don't have to. I know it's pretty weird."

I pulled a big deep breath in. "No, no," I said. "I'd *like* to do it, really."

What else could I say? Besides, it was the truth. My hands were sweating, and I didn't know how I should stand (or what to do about my sweaty hands), so I put them on my hips and tried to look real casual. I guess that I was mostly scared of how I'd seem to her. Girls — their bodies — are so much more . . . *compact*, and *organized* — know what I mean?

I closed my eyes, and she came in the room, and I could hear her walk around me, slowly. I couldn't think of anything appropriate to say. Thank God she didn't laugh. When she was going out the door, she just said, very softly, "Thanks."

After a brief debate inside my head, I made myself stay naked for my looking time. I didn't know how Dori'd handled that, but somehow it seemed proper, doing it that way. Later on, she told me she had felt — and done — the same. The Adam-and-Eve effect, I guess.

Dori'd taken my same pose: hands on hips, one foot forward, with that leg a little bent. She looked even better than I'd thought she would. I don't mean she had more of this or less of that or a better-looking whatsis. It was just the overall impression that I got. Sure, I guess I would have liked to touch her, too. But it honestly never came into my mind, until later. I was too caught up in doing what we'd said — agreed — to do. I left the bathroom, but not before I'd also said my "Thanks" — to her, to evolution and creation, and for the fact we'd gotten through another great experience together. A milestone, I should say. Then I think I closed my mouth, at last, and swallowed.

Of course I've kept that picture of her body in my mind; I doubt I'll ever lose it. It excites me and it calms me, both. The whole experience was good.

It made us better friends. And, funnily, it made me know I still had growing up to do. I wasn't ready, yet, to take responsibility for anyone as beautiful and precious as Dorinda. Heck, I wouldn't even wear my father's father's watch, for fear of losing it, or hurting it, somehow.

Anyway, back to the present; I started pedaling the bike, and she began to row.

"Why do they, anyway?" I asked. "The ones that do. Seriously."

"Do what?" said Dori, looking up at me. Her long, bare legs were beautiful, stretched out right at the end of every stroke. Both of us were sort of coasting, working the machines, but not real hard.

"Do get to be like you were saying — drunks and druggies."

"*I* don't know," she said. "But I'm pretty sure it's not because they've gotten more support than they could handle."

"Maybe they need Varney's values classes," I suggested. And yes, it's true, I let my eyes roll heavenward.

"Oh, absolutely," Dori said. "Oh, sure. You know what I think? I think people dump too much on schools and teachers. The really big and really good stuff that a person learns? They learn that in *relationships*, I think. Don't you? Not to say there aren't things that I can learn from Varney."

"You mean, like, How a Bill Becomes a Law?"

"Heck, no," said Dori. "I mean besides that sort of stuff. I mean the things you absolutely have to have — to get along, to *function* right. Parts of your philosophy of life, I guess, the way you want to *be*."

"But didn't you just say. . . ?" I made vague gestures with one hand.

"I *said* — agreed with you — that no one learns that kind of stuff in *class*," said Dori. "That doesn't mean that you can't learn it from a *teacher*, though. As long as he or she's your friend, and *you* know some relationship exists besides — *you* know — the usual."

I nodded. That made sense. I'd learned so much from both my parents, not because they *were* my parents, but because of the relationship I had with them, I think. Because of how they treated me and — I was *sure* of this — because of how they were themselves. They made me want to be like them, they were so incredibly . . . well, *kind*'s the word, so why not say it?

"I guess that's right," I said. "And because the two of us have such a good relationship, it's possible for you to learn a lot from *me*. Let's see." I scratched my head. "What wisdom shall I share with you to-day? Ah, yes." I cleared my throat. "Women have been put on earth to make their menfolk happy. So, from now on, just as soon as you get home, you slip into some — "

"Shut up," she said. "Shut up, shut up, shut up, shut up. . . ." She kept on going till she'd drowned me out. "You want to teach me something useful?" she went on. "Tell me how to cheer my father up. I'm serious."

"Well, maybe we could bring him into our exercise group," I said. "I'm sure he'd love your outfit, and especially how I can see your. . . ."

"What? My what?" said Dori, interrupting. She slipped her feet out of the straps that held them on the foot pedals, and took her hands off both the lever-oars. Then, lying back and balanced only on her fanny, she spread her arms and legs apart, looking *slightly* like an asking-for-it frog.

"You mean when I'm like *this*?" She laughed at my expression. You couldn't exactly see through her suit, but then you couldn't *not* see through it, either.

"Sober up," I told her sternly. "You're in a *gym*, you know. Go for the burn, why don't you? Look. Come on. I'll race you up to Pittsburgh." And I leaned way forward on the handlebars, picking up the pace.

"Oooh," she said. "The burn! Is that what happens when we get to Pittsburgh? And you take down my leotard, and I start squealing 'Stop, stop, stop. . . .' "

I reached way out in front of me and to the left, and flipped the TV on. Squeals now turned to outrage in the background; I turned the volume up.

I sped along now, setting quite a pace. To my right, there was the great Monongahela River, wasn't it? And to my left, for sure, Judge Wapner.

15
EDITORIAL —
THE *DUSTIN TIMES*

NO SAN FRANCISCOS HERE

The Dustin school directors and the town police have put our local youth on notice. Dustin isn't going to be another San Francisco, Amsterdam, or Rio. Not in size, thank goodness. And not in style, or attitude, the so-called "freedom" of the sixties, either.

Our response: Three Cheers for Sanity and Scruples!

Don't be deceived. Dustin's not immune to any social problem. We've had teenaged alcoholics in our town. We've also had our share of "pot-heads," and "coke-heads," and "pill-heads," and "speed freaks" here, and chances are we will again. Even the best of crops can yield bad seed. Recently, we've heard, some kids have "gotten into" crack, the latest poison fruit from off the drug tree. There is sexual activity among some teens in town. Our children have become, and gotten one another, pregnant. Our daughters have procured abortions. If it can happen anywhere, it can also happen here.

But, just as that is true, so is something else. We can, and have begun to, tell the kids of Dustin we say "No."

Three Saturdays ago, school and town authorities, alerted by concerned youngsters and their parents, broke up a massive drug-and-alcohol-related party that was taking place on public property. A few arrests were made, and many names were taken. Kids were put on notice: No. No more of this behavior. We haven't heard of any major parties since.

That doesn't mean our problems are over, though. Just last week, we heard that birth control equipment and advice were being freely, even casually, dispensed in town, some of it to teens who may see such availability as an invitation to, or countenancing of, activity. And we are not naive enough to think that kids have stopped all drug experiments inside our borders.

One observation, then, linked to a suggestion. Recent surveys have revealed that teenagers today are too immature to make a lot of choices in their lives. Indeed, they may not even want to, we are told. And so, perhaps to help them make one necessary choice, we propose the school should make some diagnostic use of tests, when there's some reason to believe a teen may be involved with drugs. Testing, as we're all aware, is an essential, useful tool of modern education. Why not use it to the fullest?

16
RESPONSE —
IN *DUST DEVILS*

To the Editor:

Yoo-hoo! Everyone! D'you read the Wednesday *Dustin Times*? The editorial: NO SAN FRANCIS-COS HERE? I don't know about all you-who, but it makes *me* think old Horace Greeley might have had some good advice* to give.

Just in case you missed the editorial, here are its main insights and suggestions:

1. What took place by the stanchion, three Saturdays ago, was "a massive drug-and-alcohol-related party."

*"Go west, young man, go west." You didn't know that?

2. If kids learn about birth control and are allowed access to condoms, diaphragms, the pill, et cetera, that'll make them think that grown-ups *want* for them to you-know-what.
3. That the school should start drug-testing on suspicion; awareness of the possibility of such tests would act as a deterrent.
4. Not only are we teens incapable of making decisions for ourselves, a lot of us don't even *want* to.

It also said the town had put us kids "on notice."

Reactions (mine, in order):

1. There must have been another Stanchion Party at another stanchion.
2. I'm sure *my* parents do: They've been after me and after me.
3. That should do a lot for our morale; and, look how grate the thret of speling tests has wurked!
4. Me, I'd hate it if my favorite band (Herr Doktor and the Unterfuehrers) made *me* say stuff about the schedule, the program, courses, speakers, the teachers, after-school activities, a teen center, hall conduct, dress, and the school athletic code. I mean, even *thinking* about making decisions about things like them has given me this awful *headache.* . . .

And here are things I think the school should do, at once, if they want to help the students even more:

a. Discontinue sexually suggestive sports, like basketball, hockey, soccer and (especially) golf.
b. Have only one kind of food served at the cafeteria each day. And, nothing spicy, please.
c. Get all the stories about that "coke-head" Sherlock Holmes out of the library, and burn all other books by people who write about, know about, or have been involved with drugs or sex or alcohol. The remaining books could be moved to the small closet at the head of the stairs, freeing up the present library space for voluntary moments of silence and the postings of further notices from the town or the Direktorship.

Respectfully submitted,
Gabriel Podesta, Junior Class

17
REACTIONS

"Dori showed me what you wrote," Llewellyn Fabb informed me in his standard, no-fun tone of voice. "Your letter in the high school paper."

"Mmmm," I said, and nodded, being just as serious as he was. I tend to do that: act like anyone I'm with at any given moment. That's either because (a) I like to put people at their ease, or (b) I play games at everyone's expense, or (c) I have no real identity or style at all, and nothing else to do, and so just mimic what's available, the way a monkey sometimes does.

It was "places everyone" in the Fabb kitchen, he on one side of the table and me on the other; one character was missing, though — our leading lady. I was clutching the base of a glass that still had about an inch of apple juice in it. Either the glass or my palm was sweating. Mr. Fabb was staring at the open book he'd shoved away when I'd come in. It was Orwell's *Animal Farm*. Dori'd said she'd meet me there at five and it was quarter past. Where was she, anyway?

"What you're doing takes a lot of *guts*," he said. That final word, and how he leaned on it, surprised me. Mr. Fabb did not use slang *or* emphasis. His style is formal somberness, like undertakers' work clothes. You remember when he said he'd like to kill *la* Brautigan? That was the only other time I'd ever heard him sound . . . *enthusiastic*.

"You know that if you cross the line one time too many, you're going to get wiped out. You know that, don't you?" He didn't raise his head to ask me that, but just his eyes. I felt as if he wanted one good peek into the back rooms of my brain, the places where I kept the stuff I really *knew*. "*Wiped out?*" He must be kidding.

"Oh, gee," I said, "it isn't that bad, is it?" I thought I sounded like the standard fourteen-year-old nerd in a failed TV pilot. And so to make things even worse, I added on a nervous laugh, the one I wish I could grow out of.

"I'm just a twerp, let's face it," I continued. "A member of the junior class. Who pays attention to a kid in high school?"

"You miss the point," he said. "Who *you* are doesn't matter in the least. You're dealing with ideo-logues. You know what that word means?"

Naturally, I nodded. Fast train on a single track.

"You're making fun of folks who don't like certain kinds of fun at all," he said. "It's as if you're mocking their religion, their most sacred set of principles. Listen to me, Gabe; here's the way they see it. Everybody knows that unplanned teenage pregnancies are bad, and so are drugs and alcohol abuse. *They* have come out strong against those things. That makes them *good*, you understand? So anything *they* say, concerning these and other subjects, is quite close to being sanctified. From good *comes* good. You see that?"

His voice had gotten louder, and his eyes were wide and . . . *snappy*. When he'd said that bit about good coming from good, he'd beaten out the words on the kitchen table with his middle finger, with the pointer finger pressed against the back of it. You *bet* I said I saw that.

"So anyone who takes another point of view, who — what did Dori call it? — *goofs* on them, that person probably is *bad*, and should be dealt with." He took a real deep breath and leaned back in his chair.

"You don't disparage zealots, Gabe," he said. "Those people don't *have* faults, they find them."

"But, wait," I said. "Kids don't grow up in vacuums. Parents here in town — they can't believe we're totally responsible for everything that happens. I mean, a lot of them have not been what I'd call red-hot examples. . . ."

As I was saying that, he threw his eyes at me again and right away I thought: oh-oh. Could he be thinking I meant him, and Dori's mother?

"Irrelevant and immaterial," he snapped. "By focusing on kids, what's wrong with kids, how they've turned out, they've managed to *assign* the blame.

Society, the schools, the movies and TV, the record industry — those things may have to *share* in it. But not themselves. They've claimed the moral high ground, Gabe."

Ah — *Terre Haute* again, I thought.

"They never even factor in their own inflexibilities and cruelties," he said, his voice now getting louder, "the crooked little things they do that their kids see and learn from."

He pushed his chair back suddenly, and rose, walked over to the sink. He turned the water on, full blast, but I still heard the sound of one of those child-proof caps snapping off a plastic bottle, and the rattle that you make when you're procuring aspirin for yourself. He ran some water in a glass and drank.

Dori was sure right. Her father had an attitude. But it was more than simple grump-grump-grump. There was an *enemy* out there. *I* thought they were jerks, but *he* thought they were dangerous. It seemed to me he'd found the perfect target for some rage he'd been repressing. Diagnosis by Podesta, G., son-of-the-psychologist.

"Well," I said, trying to lighten up the atmosphere, "my parents say this stuff just cycles in and out." He'd stayed there, standing by the sink, his back to me. "Like whether to pick up the baby when it cries. My mother says you always get an expert popping up who can prove that whatever most people are doing with kids is wrong. So, then everybody does the opposite for a while." I did my nervous ho-ho-ho's again.

"That's true up to a point," he said. He didn't

turn around, and he still sounded very agitated. But on a tighter rein. One thing I'll give the guy: He doesn't treat you like a kid, in conversations. Of course there is a bad side to that, too; maybe if he did, he might have told me to go out and play.

"But what I see happening in Dustin — here and now — alarms me," he went on. I felt my brain go slightly numb, like when you think you know, in class, exactly what the teacher's going to say.

"The righteousness, the self-satisfaction that these people seem to have. Their goddam certainty, their smugness." He was holding onto the edge of the sink, I could see, and letting his upper body sort of fall back a little ways away from it; then he'd pull himself straight up again. It amounted to a sort of rocking motion.

"The judgments they see fit to make, their general intolerance," he said. "It's that air of overall superiority that gets me, Gabe. It started when the dome went up, I swear, and there was all that national attention. As soon as this small town appeared on *60 Minutes*, well, a lot of people living here decided they were better than their neighbors — including folks in other towns, of course. The value of their homes shot up. People on the outside wanted in — what better proof of greatness is there? So pretty soon they got the big idea they'd better live up to a certain standard, too. There's this *image* you're expected to conform to, now; you know that, Gabe. You don't make too much noise; you keep your house and yard a certain way; you'd better dress just-so in shops downtown, and only *open* certain kinds of shops. It didn't used to be like that, I swear to you."

He rocked a few times more. "People weren't so damn *sure* ten years ago."

I saw his point. As the son-of-the-psychologist, I'm extra good at seeing other people's points, of course. If I were Mr. Fabb, watching other people feeling confident and smug, when I was feeling just the opposite — well, that would rankle me, no end. Heck, those people irk me as I am. I *was* the one who wrote that letter, after all.

"I guess that's ri — " I'd started when she burst into the room, her arms embracing grocery bags. How do I — G. Podesta — spell relief? D–O–R–et cetera.

"Hi, Pops. Hey, Gaberootie," Dori said. "Sorry I'm so late. But if you had seen the lines at the IGA, I swear there must be people coming into town from *Pittsburgh*. . . ."

Mr. Fabb stopped rocking, turned and put a rather ghastly smile in place, and kissed her on the cheek. Then he turned the other way, and quickly left the room.

"Censorship?" said Varney Poole. "Not really." Chew, chew, chew; swallow. "Is it?" Cut another bite. "Hmm, I guess it is."

He lifted up that thoughtful forkful of my mother's blueberry pie, and put it in his mouth, and chewed, and swallowed it. When he spoke again, his tongue was bluish black, the way a chow chow's is. A chow chow is a blocky breed of dog, from China. A chow *hound* is a stocky little social studies teacher, and American.

"But look at it another way," he said, "and you

could say they were trying to keep from getting into that — censorship, I mean." He looked across the table at my father, who had just brought up the dirty c-word.

Varney is adviser to the paper, down at school, a job for which there aren't any volunteers, I'll bet. The subject was my letters to the editor, and all the flap the last one started, Varney'd said.

"Oh, come off it, Mr. Poole," said Dori Fabb, the other dinner guest that night. "Let's say you *could* just have a 'friendly chat' with Gabe, like they suggested. And get him to agree he wouldn't write them anymore. All that is is Mister Nice Guy censorship. How's it any different from, say, cutting out selected sentences or paragraphs? The purpose and result's the same: Little Gabe gets mugged and muzzled."

I nodded, trying to look like a potential martyr, feeling very pleased inside. My letter must have touched a nerve. The school directors wanted Varney to make sure I didn't make it into print again, one way or another. As Dori'd said: That's censorship.

"I'm curious," my father said to Varney. "You say they felt you should have exercised a little more 'discretion,' was it?" Varney nodded, chewing. "Did they mention anything *specific*? Which parts you ought to have 'discretioned' out of there?"

My father smiled — that friendly, open, easygoing one that seems to fit his face so perfectly. I'm not surprised that he's the greatest putting teacher. He could teach *Bette Midler* how to putt.

"Well actually — um, *yes*, I'd say they did," said

Varney. His smile was different than my dad's. Much less secure; in this case, slightly rueful, you could say.

"Bea Teagle thought that all of Gabe's suggestions were, well . . . 'patronizing and sarcastic,' I believe she said. Or maybe it was 'snide and supercilious.' " Varney looked at me apologetically. "She said when *she* was growing up, a boy who acted fresh and rude like that would have a good long meeting with his father's razor strap. She said that she was sorry, but that she — "

" — WAS OF THE OLD SCHOOL . . ." all of us joined in to say, and Varney laughed.

"But how about . . ." my mother started. Then she stopped, re-tooled and said, "I'm curious. Were there any *other* things Gabe said that they objected to?" *My mother.* I knew exactly what she had in mind.

Varney nodded while he scraped the last of the blueberry goo from his plate with the side of his fork.

"How about another piece?" my mother said.

"That really is great pie," said Varney, passing her his plate.

"Yup," he said, when it was safely back in front of him, re-loaded, "there was some sentiment against his . . . well, his mentioning those different kinds of birth control, right in the student paper. Mr. Nevins pointed out that Channel 8 won't even take an ad for them, because of their offensiveness to certain people. He asked how I could justify doing almost the same thing for free that a private corporation wouldn't even do for *money*."

"Wow," my mother said. She whistled. "Telling *point*," she said, and nodded, pseudo-thoughtfully. "Any other zingers?"

Varney had to swallow hastily. "Well, naturally they didn't like 'Herr Doktor and the Unterfueh-rers.' " He got that out while dabbing with his napkin. "That was 'darn near bordering on slander,' Mr. Nevins thought."

"But Mr. Poole," I whined, "the last time, I said 'troika' and I called the school a 'gulag.' Don't you think that shows I'm politically impartial — or, possibly, just kidding? Of course, to them it *could* mean I'm confused, or ignorant."

"I don't know about that," said Varney, "but there did seem to be some question in their minds about your general . . . stability. They asked me if I thought your elevator stopped at all the floors — or Dr. Leeds did, anyway. That took me by surprise, I must admit."

Dori howled with glee and bounced a little in her chair.

"And what did *you* say, Mr. Poole?" she asked. "Did you refuse to answer, maybe? Plead a previous derangement? How would *you* have answered, Mrs. P?" She'd turned toward my mother. "You're a mental health professional."

My mother narrowed up her eyes and stared at me, one pointer finger leaning on her cheek, the thumb beneath her chin.

"It's kind of hard to say," she said, real slowly. "Not without a lot of testing, first." She licked her lips. "Suppose we try some word associations." I nodded, most enthusiastically, the perfect subject.

"I'll say a word, and you reply with the first thing that comes into your mind, all right? Ready?"

"*Sex!*" I snapped. I beamed and held one finger up. Score one for sanity, my gesture clearly said.

"No," she said, "I — "

"*Sex!*" I answered, quicker than a flash. I nodded as I smiled, this time.

"Look — " she started, hanging in there.

"*Sex!*" I cried, with cheerful virtuosity. Three cheers for me!

Dori started making gagging sounds; my mother wig-wagged both hands: time out.

"What's the matter?" I looked back and forth at both of them and pretended to be puzzled. "A little bit *too* normal, am I, hmmm? You don't like it when I have the one thing on my mind that everybody knows is all that boys my age have on their minds? Is that it, hmmm?" I fixed my stare on my mother. "What kind of a psychologist are you, anyway?"

My mother, who's in practice, just ignored me and turned back to Varney.

"Anyway," she said, "getting back to birth control" — I stayed in character and nodded cheerfully — "I must say *I* resented that word 'casually,' a lot. In the editorial, I mean. Where they said we 'even casually' dispensed it. I'm assuming they meant us, at the clinic."

"That's such a crock," said Dori. "When *I* went in, the nurse practitioner talked me out of even *holding hands*, as soon as she found out who I was going with."

"There it is again — harrassment," my father said to me, completely straight-faced. "First the cops,

95

and now the nurse practitioners. Everybody's out to get you, Gabe."

"*Your* problem," I told my mother, ignoring him *and* Dori, "is you don't do what Dr. Leeds did in our class: Tell the kids that sex outside of marriage is completely *wrong*. Or do you? You never told *me* that, exactly." I paused and scratched my head. "Or *did* you?"

"He thinks he's being funny," Dori told my mother. "He knows exactly what you said, what you both said; he even told me what it was and didn't ruin it." She turned toward my father — so he'd know he was included, I suppose. "It was some of the neatest stuff I ever heard. I wish that every parent in the world could talk to kids like that. And also, need I add" — she grinned and shot a glance at me, and one at Varney — "Doc Discomfort."

We burst out laughing and of course the parents clamored for enlightenment. The three of us obliged them.

It had happened in the third of Varney's values classes. The subject was "self-discipline," and guess what? Instead of reading an opening essay, Varney introduced "a most distinguished visitor" (he swears he didn't wink on that), who'd "lead today's discussion." It was old Earring-Head himself, and pretty soon it got to be real clear he had one aspect of self-d in mind, and only one, the part a person uses to refrain from having sex.

"It was weird," said Dori to my mother. "He started out with, like, this little rap about . . . well, *you*. Not you, specifically, of course — but people in your field. 'Sex educationists,' he called you. He told us — real sarcastically, I thought — how you want the kids you see to be real 'comfortable' with their decision. About, well, whether, they indul — "

"Wait. Back up." I interrupted her. "What he said *before* that was" — I said this to my mother — "that you people tell the kids they've got a lot of *choices*. And then you *describe* the choices. He said a lot of times you'll even give the kids a lot of real good reasons *not* to do it."

"Like you did with him," said Dori, nodding in this kid's direction. She wasn't joking, either; this was serious.

"Ri-i-ight," my mother slowly said. "We always do, with everyone. But isn't Leeds against kids having sex? Of course he is. He must be. You just said so."

"Absolutely," Varney said. "But, like Gabe said, *he's* against it just because it's *wrong*. That means, to him, there *isn't* any choice. And he believes that everyone should sell that point of view."

"Good *luck*," my father said. "That wouldn't be much harder, I don't guess, than selling smoked salami in Pompeii."

"Wait a minute," said my mother. "Turn the picture back again. Dr. Leeds is saying that the right choice isn't comfortable? That doing what you should do won't feel good?"

"He certainly *implied* that," Dori said. "But when we asked, just like you did, right straight out, he said he wasn't saying that. Necessarily. He said he only meant that whether it was comfortable or not had nothing to do with the case." Dori smiled. "And then he said the right choice often does cause real discomfort for a person."

"So, of course that fool Deano had to ask Dr. Leeds if the discomfort some teenagers felt from not having sex was good for them or not," I said. "And after everyone had stopped being crazy, Leeds said it certainly wouldn't do them any harm. So, of course Arby asked if that was a medical opinion or a psychological one, and Dr. Leeds said 'Both.' "

"I don't know." My mother shook her head. "Manipulating someone's wrong. Hurting someone's wrong. Lying to them, using them. Screwing someone's life up. All those things are wrong. And so can having sex be wrong, in *or* out of marriage."

She stopped and looked embarrassed.

"Listen to me. Woman on the soapbox. Bringing work home from the office. Sorry," she said. She shook her head again. "I just don't like it when a person passes judgment on a thing that can't be judged except in context. To tell a kid that sex is always wrong, except in marriage. . . ." She smiled a little twisted smile.

"*I* wouldn't even try," said Varney. "Aside from feeling like a hypocrite — "

"Why, Mr. *Poole!*" said Dori automatically, widening her eyes. But then she dropped her eyes and matched his blush. "Sorry," she just managed, in a mutter. "That was just about as immature of me as. . . ."

"The thing *I* want to know," my father started in his loud let's-change-the-subject tone of voice, "is how come *you*" — he had his eyeballs on his son —

"didn't tell us all this stuff before? Have you become secretive, as you approach your late-ish middle teens?" He grinned, while winking at my mother.

"Frankly, Dad," I phoneyed back at him, "I was afraid this sort of talk would only make you both uncomfortable. And may I add I've found my choice a good one? I've been *very* comfortable with it."

That, of course, made Dori and my mother boo and hiss, and throw their napkins at my head, not hard. Varney seized the moment: slid the pie plate over by his place, and cut himself another little sliver.

18
GETTING TOLD

I got the note first thing in the morning, typed on a prescription pad. "Please report to Dr. Leeds's office directly after your lunch period." It was signed by either Fabian Leeds or Zulem Soobr.

I showed it to Lafountain in the hall.

"Interesting," he said. "Note the time of day. Probably they want to do some tests on you."

"Tests?" I said. I stared at his agreeably geeky face; I didn't comprehend. "Tests to find out what?"

"Oh — how does the high school food affect a proven loser? That kind of thing," he said. "Is there any *further* loss of function?"

"So, what'll I have to do, d'you think?"

"I don't know," he said. "Probably they'll make you close your eyes and see if you can touch the tip of your nose with a nasturtium. Or have you strip and walk a balance beam with Jello on your head. Pretty much the same old standards."

"Oh, shucks," I said. "*I* was guessing that the school directors wanted . . . well, some further input on the *issues* that I raised. How I felt about lacrosse, perhaps — or Scott Fitzgerald."

"No," Lafountain said. "Varney was just sucking up to your parents when he told you all that stuff. No one *cares* what you think, Gabe. This'll be about the food, you'll see. Maybe they'll ask you some multiple-choice toughies. Check one: Is the high school food, like, (a) less filling, or does it merely (b) taste great?"

But *during* lunch that day, I discovered that Lafountain was mistaken, once again. People *did* care what I thought. Rotten Ronnie Gervais cared.

Ronnie'd changed a lot since kindergarten — physically, that is. What once had been an agile, squeaky, snapping little wharf rat of a kid had been transformed by time and free weights in his Uncle Archibald's garage into a kind of water buffalo. Nowadays, he glared a lot, and flexed, and drove a black and shiny van. Now and then, he'd charge, and stomp somebody good.

"Lemme tell you something," he suggested, as he sat down in the cafeteria, right across from me.

"You're a wiseass," he continued, "with those letters in the paper and that shit." He wore designer jeans, a tan safari jacket (belted and with epaulets, the belt just tied), and two gold chains around his neck. *Everybody* knew Naomi Leh had given him the slender one, with the small gold #1 that hung there in the hollow of his throat.

"You know what that shit makes me think?" he asked. "It makes me think you're either, like, some dumb shit Commie, or a dealer, or a pervert who's molestin' younger kids. Either way, that's someone who's a fuck-up, who's messing with a way of life I happen to enjoy."

I didn't go to spoken language, at that point. Instead, I stuck to simple and preverbal signs: a smile, added to the gestures that said "Me?" and "Don't be silly!"

Ronnie wasn't reading, though.

"You dealing drugs, Podesta?" he went on. "Usin' them for bait with little kids? You know what that can get you, don't you? That can get you broken up in ways you won't believe."

He paused, just staring, while he pulled some further thoughts together. Then he pointed at my face, while saying, "Listen up and listen good. The day my *sister* tells me she — or any of her friends — have had to, like, say 'No' to *you* . . . You'll wish you never saw that day, I promise you."

For saying "No" to *Ronnie* (Dori'd told me), Lori Mason had been pushed out of his van at one A.M., way the hell and gone out in West Ellington, on some dirt road. One of Ronnie's friends had told him she'd put out. That meant that Ronnie didn't have to treat her like a "*good* girl"; she was just a pig, a slut. Ronnie thought that every female human being in his age group was a "*good* girl" or a "slut." Only category A was "matrimonial material." I'd heard him say that. When it came to marriage, Ronnie said, he wasn't taking any "sloppy seconds." This was the moral arbiter who didn't want his sister dealing, or *not* dealing, with the likes of me.

I'm pretty sure I muttered that I wasn't into drugs *or* juveniles, as everybody knew, and that I'd match my devotion to the free enterprise system with his or anybody else's. And as far as writing letters (I almost surely said), it was still a free country until Mr. Morehead and the school directors said it wasn't.

To which *he* said, "Fuckin' right," and "Just remember you been told," and left my table.

As, moments later, I sped down the corridors toward Leeds's office, I must admit to having paranoia flashes. "*Et tu*, Ronnie?" came into my brain, unbidden. That Leeds was not a fan of mine was understandable, but weren't kids supposed to stick together?

"Once upon a time, *I* was a rebel, too," said Dr. Leeds to me, confidingly. I think he thought that he could come down to my level. "Can you believe that, Gabe?"

We'd taken up positions in his office. He'd been behind the big executive-type desk when I came in, but after we shook hands, he'd come around and curled up in the easy chair. I think *he* thought that this was how we always sat, the people in my age group. I thought he looked ridiculous: all bones and glare and angles.

He'd left me with the sofa. I sat up straight and crossed a leg and tried to look adult. This once, I wasn't going to "monkey-do" what I was seeing. I guess I purely didn't trust this man.

"I don't think I *am* a rebel, Dr. Leeds," I said, "although I've heard my mother say that it's a stage a lot of guys go through." I decided I'd pretend he wasn't a physician. Doctors are too scary, always with their clothes on, telling you to cough and stuff. I'd pretend that he was something else . . . a golfer, maybe. Or better yet, Lafountain.

"Of course it's also true that all the *world's* a stage," I added. It's possible I winked as well, as if the two of us were fellow mischief-makers. I had no plan. I simply reached for what was there, and used it. That worked when I was dealing with Lafountain.

He looked a little startled. It was probably the wink, if I *did* wink. I'm really not too sure. But then he pulled himself together.

"And all the men and women merely actors, isn't it?" he said. "But you don't strike me as a real *bad* actor, Gabe. I've looked you up; I've got a line on you."

He reached behind him, to the desktop, found a folder there and opened it. More nods. I guessed what might be coming next, an f-word: flattery.

"You're *very* bright," he said. "I never had your scores, I promise you. You should have quite a future. Here or anywhere."

"Well, I hope so," I agreed. Throw my scores up at me, would he? I'd fix *him*. "That's one thing a person can look forward to, I always say, the future. Don't you think so, sir?"

"Er, yes," said Leeds. He took another peek inside my folder. "But what I can't make heads or tails of,"

104

he continued, "is why you've cast yourself as our antagonist — meaning Mr. Nevins, Mrs. Teagle and myself — starting back before we got in office, even. Would you care to *tell* me why?"

"No, not really," I replied, going to the plain, unvarnished truth.

Leeds's mouth came open, slightly, but he didn't speak. But then he smiled — a sly, I-get-it, *youthful* sort of smile.

"I understand," he said. "But *would* you, anyway?"

"Well," I said, "if you insist." I took a breath. "That corny slogan drove me up the wall. The one you had on all your signs? L-O-Vee-Hee-love, and all that stuff? It seemed so chauvinistic and simplistic. Not to mention totally nonsensical." I rolled a hand toward him, palm up.

"Did it now?" said Leeds. And as he did, his cheekbones got a spot of color in them, underneath that tight and smoothly shaven skin. "*I* didn't think so, when I wrote it. And neither did the people when they voted, did they?"

"No," I said, "but, hey: 'The people is a beast.' "

My father'd told me the year before that getting in the first quote counts for quite a lot in any upscale argument. I'd managed that, way back, with "all the world's a stage," and here was number two. I could see that Leeds was stung by this small beauty. "*The people is a beast.*" The "is" in it is such a pisser. The fact that it *sounds* wrong is what makes it magnificent. Because by sounding wrong, it also sounds authentic. Plus, most people don't know who said it and assume that it's someone like Marie Antoinette instead of Alexander Hamilton, which puts a whole different light on it, he being a kind of founding father, and all. I think that doctors, as a rule, are pretty weak on quotes, anyway, except for ones they learn in med school. For instance: "Take two shut-up pills and call me in the morning."

"Possibly. Sometimes," said Leeds, staying in the safety zone. "But I hardly need remind you that our Constitution puts a different light on it." He looked up at the ceiling. He might as well have put a sign up: QUOTE AHEAD. " 'So that government of the people, by the people, and for the people, shall not perish from this earth,' " he finished, grandly.

"Lincoln said that, sir," I said. "That's from the Gettysburg Address." I wondered why it is that people who abuse the Bill of Rights always seem to try to quote the Constitution.

"*Good* for you," said Leeds. "Of *course* it is!" He'd hardly missed a beat. "I couldn't sneak one by you, could I? Excellent. You're sharp, all right; I want you on our side, Podesta."

For a moment there I thought that he was going to reach way out in my direction, offer me a hand to shake. Like podners. But I also felt that we were getting close to crunch time. *Tempus* was a-*fugit*ting, and Leeds would not assign good patient time to kids like G. Podesta.

"I hope that Mr. Poole got that idea across," he said. "That we have common goals, that we're together on this thing." (*Thing?* I wondered — *thing?* What *thing* was that, I wondered.) "That there's nothing for a guy like you to be upset about, in what the school is doing." (Ah! The whole entire *thing*, it was, from A for Anything the school directors — and the town police — proclaimed was best for kids to Z for Zapping any kid who disagreed.)

"Well," I said, "if that's the case, you won't object if I keep writing letters to the paper. I mean, if we have common goals, like you just said, the chances are that you'll agree with most of what I write."

I smiled, and then, because I couldn't help myself, I blinked my eyes at him — just batted them a time or two, or maybe half a dozen.

That did it; I had finally gone too far, by far. Leeds uncoiled himself and leaned in my direction, both feet on the floor.

"Look," he said, his tone of voice no longer buddy-buddy. Not even doctor-patient, now. Doctor-*nurse*? you ask. Perhaps. "Let's cut the fencing and get down to cases. You want to see this high school full of drunks and junkies?"

Yes, clearly Dr. Leeds was out of patience. Talking *Means* requires patience; he was going to segue right to *Ends*. Me? I still had patience by the carload.

"Gee," I said. "*This* high school?" I made the all-around-us gesture. "Drunks and junkies? Here? No, I guess I don't, if you're going to put it that way."

"And I don't imagine," he went on, but now sarcastically, "that you'd like to have a lot of pregnant women in your classes. Or people with AIDS? Or various other kinds of moral defectives? Or traitors to your country?"

"Moral *detectives*?" I said. What the hay — I might as well have fun. "Like members of the vice squad?

Tubbs and Crockett? Wow — but no, I'm pretty sure I wouldn't go for that. Not in my *classes*, anyway."

Traitors to my country? I was thinking. *Dori? Deano Dobbins? Me?*

"Okay," said Leeds. He got up from his chair. "Okay, I've had it." The atmosphere had changed again. He took a real deep breath, then pinched his bloodless lips together.

"I can see I'm wasting my breath talking sense and reason to a person of your ilk, Podesta. I've got half a mind to just suspend you, here and now," he said. "Maybe Mrs. Teagle has the right idea about how to handle little snots like you."

All of a sudden, it had gotten to be the way it was when *Ronnie* told me what the score was, except in this case I felt different. Ronnie hadn't been Authority. I was used to Ronnie; I'd grown up with him. And Ronnie was a kid, like me.

Hearing Leeds, my heart began to pound. I got this wet, full feeling in my chest, as if I couldn't take a real deep breath. I was being bullied. I was scared and mad and also close to tears — of anger, I should add, not fear or sorrow.

"Let me tell you something, Mr. Gabriel Podesta, member of the junior class." Leeds was going on, looking down at me and pointing, just like Ron. Getting told involves a lot of getting pointed at, apparently. "Maybe you can dance your little dialectic rings around the teachers in this high school, but I've got news for you. All that arrogant and self-important sass won't get you anywhere with me.

You want trouble, mister, you are going to get it — by the truckload."

"Well, let me tell *you* something, Dr. Leeds," I said, standing up myself. I gulped air down, but still my voice was not the drill instructor's bark I wanted. The darned thing sounded strained and muffled — weenie-ish. I just hoped it wouldn't crack. I'd never spoken to a grown-up in this way, before.

"I didn't *have* to come and talk to you, today. You aren't on the staff of Dustin High. You have no power over me. And when it comes to saying what is right and wrong about the way this school — or this whole town — is run, we're *equals*, Dr. Leeds. And all your threats and bullying attempts won't get you anywhere with *me*."

With that, I double-timed it out the door, before I had a heart attack. Behind me, Leeds was shouting something, getting in a few last words. Because of doors and distance, I missed most of them, but there were four I caught all right and, yes, they bothered me.

"Blah-blah-blah-blah-blah," he said, *"you cheeky little junkie."*

19
WEIRD CONNECTIONS

My mother's mother's birthday is October 21.

Which meant that, seeing as my dad was out of town, my mother needed *me* to go pick up the sundial that she'd ordered from the garden shop for her mother's birthday present, but which didn't come and didn't come until three days before the day itself.

Which meant I had to first go by my mother's office, after school, in order to pick up the check that she'd forgotten to make out at breakfast.

Which meant I met the letter carrier outside the clinic door with that day's mail.

Which meant he handed it to me instead of slotting it.

Which meant I saw the envelope on top and mentioned to my mom that it looked pretty strange, and so she went "Unh-huh," and opened it.

She read its contents quickly, then a second time, then sighed. I think my mom is very beautiful. She has enormous, deep-set eyes and long dark hair, and usually she looks as if she'd slept ten solid hours in the month of May. But she is also vulnerable. She suffers with whoever's hurting, in whatever way. Now she looked at me — I'm sure my face was one big question mark — and nibbled at her lower lip before she tossed the thing across the desk in my direction.

"These come from time to time," was all she said. I'd grabbed the letter and was reading it.

It could have been made up of bits cut out of magazines or newspapers; it was that *genre* — that type — for sure. This one, though, was done in pencil, printed out on five-hole, wide-lined, note-book paper.

> *So now your handing rubbers out to all the queers. That makes us flaming mad. So see you soon. No fooling.*

20
ILLUMINATIONS

Thursday nights, the clinic's open in the evenings, too. Once I'd seen that note, I wasn't all that wild about my mother being down there after sundown. It seemed to me that anyone insane enough to firebomb a building would prefer that time of day. I mean, it's hard to skulk around in broad daylight, with lots of other people in the streets. Firebombers always "skulk," I think. And this one might be so loony that he wouldn't even notice that the clinic wasn't empty, this one night. I just assumed it was a "he." Oily rags and gasoline, or timing fuses — all of them say "guy," to me.

But she, my mother, wouldn't listen to my protests. She said, "Put yourself in *my* place. I do the duty rosters. Could *you* leave *your*self off, on Thursday nights?"

Dori called to say she'd like to study at *mi casa*, that same *noche*. A major Spanish test was coming up and I was psyched. Because we'd sort of dawdled over supper, I'd managed to convince my mom to let me drive her down in her car, and drop her at the clinic. That way, I could pick up Dori, bring her back to our place and then also take her home again before collecting Mom. I think my mother liked my having company, so she could feel she hadn't left me by my lonesome. With my father on the road a lot, she puts some extra pressure on herself.

Dori must have been outside already, waiting on the little kitchen porch when I pulled up. I'd only barely stopped and — whoosh! — the door flew open and she flopped inside.

I noticed she came empty-handed.

"Forgetting something?" I inquired. I hadn't turned the motor off.

"No. Let's go," she said, just staring out the windshield, straight ahead.

"No books? No notebook? Not so much as a verb wheel, even? You aren't going to *estudiar por el Señor* Maduro's little inquisition, after all? Look — just because my mother's out, that doesn't mean that you can . . . have your way with me. I've told you and I've told you: I'm saving it for — "

"Gabe," she said. "Just drive the car, all right? I'll use your stuff if I deci — "

"Oh, no you won't," said Mr. Oblivious. "I've got to study for that test myself, and — "

"Oh, God," she said, and dropped her face into her hands. "Please, let's get *out* of here, okay? Just

113

please." The last of that was muffled; I could have even heard a sob. I got the car in gear and pulled away, throwing one quick glance back at the house. Not that I was anxious for a glimpse of what — or, make that *who* — had got her so upset. Assumption by Podesta, G.

Dori had her moods but hardly ever cried. I know I mentioned her crying when she told me about confronting Brautigan, and how she said she'd cried when she *had* the confrontation. But those were about the only other times I remember, except for at the end of *Out of Africa* and that old Gary Cooper-Ingrid Bergman *For Whom the Bell Tolls* — and those two saddies cracked *me* up, as well.

Now, feeling as perceptive as a Brillo pad, I zipped my lip and drove the car, as I'd been asked to in the first place. Three minutes later, we were parked outside *my* kitchen door. Dori'd gotten a Kleenex from the glove compartment, and she blew her nose.

"Sorry. Don't know what came over me," she said. "Except of course I do." She put a hand out on my arm. She hadn't touched her seat belt yet.

"Look," she said. "D'you think that maybe we could take a little drive, before we go inside?"

"Sure, I guess," I said. Part of me still dreamed a dream *muy imposible*: an A+ on the Spanish test. "To where?"

"It doesn't matter," Dori said. "Just so it's out of town. You remember where we had that picnic by the river? Unless you think that that's too far."

It really wasn't far at all. You take the highway, not toward Ellington, the other way, toward Belden, heading out into the country. The only trouble was that it was raining, out from under Lid.

We kept on going, anyway. The rain was not that hard, nor was it cold outside. When we got to the parking space near the river, Dori got out and I followed her. We walked across the corner of what once had been a field of corn and made it to the riverbank. It was pretty dusky out there then, but we could watch the water flow. And did, a lot of it. Dori didn't jump *or* speak, and so I didn't, either. This was her excursion; I was just the company. We were getting wet, so I pretended we were Scottish, and we didn't mind. We were used to rain like this, this lovely lass and I, standing on the bank of this fast-rushing burn. I imagined that we had our dog with us, a little border collie.

After a certain while, she turned and shook some water droplets from her hair. Then she walked right up into my face. Naturally, I wrapped my arms around her.

This was a Type-A hug, the kind you (also) give your mother, or a child — and your dad as well, if you're Podesta, G. It means a lot: *I'm here*; *I absolutely care*. It isn't on the way to anywhere; it simply is. For the person needing it, this type of hug is like a fortress; you feel safe in it, you can relax, at last. If I couldn't get, and give, a Type-A hug from time to time, I think I'd be a different sort of person. Maybe more like Mr. Fabb. And that's a pretty scary sort of thought.

Dori made some letting-go sounds, up against my chest. A moment later, we were walking hand-in-hand, back to the car and into it.

"I think he's losing it," she said. There wasn't any doubt who "he" was.

"Huh," I answered. I wanted to sound interested, but uncommitted — even skeptical. I didn't want to hear her say Llewellyn Fabb was nuts. Not because I hadn't thought so, sort of, since . . . forever. But because I didn't want it to be so. I had an "Oh, come *on*," just waiting in the wings. Meanwhile, I'd said "Huh," meaning, like, "So tell me more."

Apparently, she bought it.

"He's raving constantly," she said. "The same old broken record. He says hypocrisy is rampant and that liberty's in peril, that the town is being 'pasteurized, homogenized, and polarized' — as if that combination's possible. That they're using the drug problem as a way to justify their crackdown on the kids. He says they want to turn us into clones of theirs: cunning little fat-cat, selfish rascals."

"Well, that isn't *altogether* crazy . . ." I began.

"But what he's doing," Dori said, "is kind of *ov-er*doing that and — this is really awful — taking drugs himself. Can you believe it? He gets himself, like, totally worked up, and then he pops his pills to get calmed down. So far, it's mostly Valiums, I think. When I was doing wash the other day, I found some in a little plastic thing, right in the pocket of his shirt."

"Lots of people do that, though," I said. Valium. I'd thought that it was aspirin. But Valium was not that scary, didn't have to be. "It doesn't mean . . ." I started; then I stopped. I could see her head was shaking, really hard. I could see it out of the corner of my eye.

116

"There's more," she said. "He's drinking, too. Again." She turned on the car radio, then quickly shut it off. "Yesterday, I started doing countertops. Don't I sound domestic, all this washing-cleaning crap? Anyway, I opened up the cabinet that's underneath the kitchen sink. To get the Comet, right? That's where I found a Smirnoff bottle, not half full. I'm sure it wasn't there two days ago. Well, I confronted him, of course. I told him that he better not be mixing alcohol and downs. He said he wasn't *really* using either one. Once in a month of Sundays, maybe just a pill, to help him get to sleep."

"How'd he explain the vodka, then?"

She gave a little grunt.

"Said he found it in the *library*," she said, "and brought it home and shoved it underneath the sink, just to put it somewhere. He said he thought the head librarian might blame it on the kids, unless he snuck it out of there. Which, of course, is utter bullshit. You know Ms. Johansson, and how nice she is."

"You're pretty sure he's drinking it," I said.

"Yes, really sure. I really am." She took a big deep breath. "You see, he used to drink before. Before my mother left."

"Whoa," I said. At that point, I was simply trying to process all this stuff, and also drive the car. "You knew he used to . . ." I was babbling, just filling empty air. I shook my head.

"I guess," she said. "Oh, yeah. I heard stuff going on, some nights. I more or less pretended it was something else, it wasn't what it was." Her voice took on an edge. "I still don't get it, totally. My

mom was always sweet to me. Pops was always
. . . well, just Pops. He never was the kind to show
a lot of feelings, not to me, at least. Till lately,
anyway, I *should* say. I really think he may be losing
it," she said, again.

I took a peek at her. Her eyes had gotten shiny.
I groped for her left hand and found it, held it, as
I drove. I tried to think of something positive to say.
Her father *could* be sick. I wished he'd start going
down and talking to my mother, instead of staying
home and making life miserable for Dori, popping
downs and drinking vodka, going crazy.

Crazy? Wowie-zowie. I felt the steering wheel go
slick inside my driving hand, and so I slid the other
out of Dori's grasp. Her father hadn't spouted any
craziness concerning *gays*, or AIDS, or *condoms*, had
he? I was trying to remember. I was pretty sure he
never had, to me. But he sure was the kind of guy
you read about in those "mad bomber" stories — "a
quiet sort of guy" the neighbor always says, after
he's been taken into custody.

"He's got these books about explosives . . ." Dori
was saying. She was dabbing at her eyes with that
balled-up Kleenex. I'd *heard* her, but the words had
not been registering. You know how that happens,
when your mind's on other things. I had to say what
Dori'd said inside my head before I got it. And it
freaked me out, of course.

"What?" I said. "Explosives? Books about *explosives?*"

"Take it *easy*," Dori said. I must have said that
last too loud. She touched my arm. "He isn't going
to blow us up. They're just some books and pam-

118

phlets that he got." Her voice was nearly normal, now. "Not from the library. I think he sends away for them."

"But yikes," I said. "I know this is ridiculous, but I'll just tell you. My mom just got a bomb threat — at least I'm pretty sure it was." I told her all about the note, and all. "Not that *he* . . . I mean, I'm sure. . . ."

Of course I wasn't, though. Dori calmly said her father'd often said good things about the clinic, and that she'd never heard him coming down on gays. If anything, the opposite, she said. She gave me some examples. I felt better. She said, with just a little laugh, she thought he'd be more apt to plant a bomb in Brautigan's new Escort.

"Last week, he asked me if they got another coach, if I'd play then. I told him 'Maybe,' without thinking." And now she really did laugh. "I figured that he meant next year, or something."

"But — did you ask him why he had the books and stuff?" I still was curious. A guy like him, you'd want to know. "Seems to me you ask him stuff like that — I mean, you *would*."

"Sure I did," she said. "And he just passed it off — real easily. Simple curiosity, he said. He said he'd seen some news thing on TV, where they were doing demolition on this row of old abandoned tenements. He said he'd wondered how they dropped them right in place like that; he thought that was amazing. Last year, all he'd read was laser weapons and those different things in *Star Wars*; now, he's into high explosives. He's always reading up on something; *you* know that."

"Um," I said. It was a fact. Mr. Fabb had lots of curiosity. He'd started as a physics major back in college (he had told me once), but then he'd switched to "books in general." "There's so much more than physics that excites me," he had said.

"I guess it's all this weird stuff going on," I said to Dori, then. We'd reached our driveway once again, and I'd pulled into it. As we got out, I told her about my talk with Leeds and him calling me a junkie at the end of it.

We went into the kitchen, had some pecan chocolate chips, with milk, then kept on going to the den, with me still jabbering away. By then, I was telling her about how Ronnie Gervais also took his shots at Gabe — cool Ron, another self-appointed member of the vice squad.

She had to laugh at that one.

"Ronnie?" We had flopped down on the couch. "Telling you to not go messing with his *sister*? She's in sixth grade, Gabe."

"His sister *and* her friends," I said. "By the time both him and Leeds were through with me, I felt as if I'd had a bull's-eye sweatshirt on, I swear."

Dori looked concerned, but still her eyes were twinkling.

"You better watch it, Gabe," she said. "I wouldn't want those people messin' with my lucky piece. Accent on the *piece*, that is." She licked her lips. "My *talisman*." And then she *really* smiled at me, and sent her eyebrows zooming up, like: "*Well. . . ?*"

I didn't need Miss Manners to advise me. Instinctively, I flung an arm around her shoulders and I kissed her. She kissed me back, with great intensity,

120

her open mouth alive with wet enthusiastic welcome. But, seconds later, she had pulled it back, was speaking words, out loud.

"Your shirt is soaking, still," she said, her fingers plucking at my collar.

"Yours, too," I said. "Maybe we should just. . . ."

I pulled away from her and, this one time, my fingers on the buttons of her shirt were quick as a magician's.

"Good idea," she said, returning me the favor, maybe even faster. "We wouldn't want to catch our deaths on top of . . . Ooh — oh, Gabe."

The last of that was said because, by then, we'd pushed each other's shirts down off each other's shoulders, and I had dipped my hands and face in her (adorable) bare-chestedness, where I was busily inhaling fragrances, and tasting/feeling tender, precious treasures.

"You *woman*," were the words I gasped, perhaps absurdly, thinking some huge row of *yeses*. "Yes" to her a hundred times, and to the ways our different bodies were, and worked; "yes" to that my Levis were a size or two too small.

She held my head and let me go on kissing there; she made some heartfelt sounds. And when I looked up in her eyes (still cupping both her small and cheerful breasts), she looked more proud and happy than I'd ever seen her.

"Mark the day," I said to her, and laughed. "Oh, Lord." I guess I was ecstatic. I felt crazy, full of laughter, loving, wanting — pure delight. I felt that what was happening was epic and momentous. Crazy, I both wanted to go on *and* stop to celebrate:

121

write some music, build a float, paint Dorinda's portrait, rip off all my clothes and flex my muscles, fall down on my knees. I did the last of those, flopping off the couch in front of her, still holding her around the waist. I put my head down in her lap.

It's hard to say exactly what was happening, right then — to tell you, truthfully, about what happened and what didn't happen, next. It's possible that I unbuttoned Dori's pants, then mine. I'm pretty sure that isn't any of your business.

I know the line "It isn't time" is vague to some and unacceptable to others. It draws replies like "You don't love me," or "You're just a chicken" (or "a baby/fag/tease/bastard/bitch"). But frankly — and regardless of what anybody says — knowing that it isn't time (yet) calls for lots more self-awareness, love and even (yes) *maturity* (and maybe luck) than fucking does. I think that's provable; I kid you not. Look around; observe the heartbreaks and mistakes; tell me just how smart or how together those kids were. (All this is easier, by far, to say when you are fully dressed, alone.)

So, you have doubtless guessed by now that we — both she and I — were lucky and aware (mature, in love) enough to know it wasn't time for us, just yet. Our "no" had not a thing to do with Dr. Leeds's certainties concerning right and wrong, or AIDS, or with people on TV whose own judgments on a lot of other things had never seemed us to be so hot and who were telling kids that saying "no" was what they *ought* to do.

And so we huffed and puffed a while (you can guess, imagine, any other things you like), and after that we got back fully dressed (including clean shirts from my dresser drawer) and studied Spanish, slightly dreamily, until a quarter after nine.

(One other thing, before I leave "it isn't time." Some weeks before, Dori and I *had* met a practical "condition" that my parents talked to me about: We'd had a frank and lengthy conversation on "that subject," contraception. Part of my mother's rap was this: For most people, it's much easier to make love than to talk about contraceptives. So, she said, if you *can't* do the second, you're not ready to do the first. Well, we'd talked, Dori and I had, feeling pretty darn *mature* in one case, I can guarantee you. And because in neither case was there a motion that we should begin, at once, "an active sex life" [as it's called], we [or really *she*] decided that she wouldn't start The Pill. Which meant that if there ever was a when, we'd go with what Lafountain'd started calling "the ultimate In-thing," the condom. I'd even left my mother a note at the clinic one day, asking her to bring me home a few. "Just so I can more or less see how they work," I'd written her.

"Satisfy my curiosity," she'd said to me that night. "Could you ask the pharmacist for these, at Ruskin's? *Would* you?"

"Umm, ah, yes — I think," I said, and smiled. "But luckily for me I'll never have to. You see, my mother's sort of like those ladies in the supermarket who give out samples, like of brand-new breakfast drinks, or little cocktail sausages . . . *you* know."

She tried to bat me with whatever journal she was holding, but she missed.)

So at a quarter after nine, as I just said, we climbed

back in the car again. I was feeling *very* mellow. Being with the woman that you love, being close and all with her, does something for a man that nothing else can do. Of course I don't know how it is for girls, exactly, but as a guy, you just feel . . . well, *complete*. Some word like that. It isn't quite "secure," and slightly different than a mere "all *right*," and on a higher plane than "satisfied," I'd say. *This* sounds so "mellow" that it almost makes me sick. But maybe *you* know what I'm trying to say.

I rolled up to the stop sign at the corner, going maybe 5 or 10. No lights were visible from either side, and so I rolled on through. Almost at once, the first parked car on Maple Street, the street that I'd just crossed, lit up: high-beam headlights first, then flashing double zingers on the roof. Its siren made one little growly sound, as it turned left behind me; by then, I'd reached the curb and almost stopped. Hardly what you'd call a car chase.

This was the first time in my driving life (now five months old) the cops had ever stopped me, and my heart began to pound. I tried to think if I'd been told the proper etiquette. Let's see — I knew I shouldn't wrap my license in a fifty dollar bill. . . .

I decided that the thing *to* do was probably to get right out, to leave my car. That seemed *respectful*. Staying, sitting, *slouching* in the driver's seat while being lectured by The Law — that struck me as more surly, *sulky* even. Also, maybe voluntary standing-up might tend to show the officers I *could*. People who are drunk (or anything) surely wouldn't want to advertise that fact. And maybe, if I got outside, they wouldn't even notice Dori. It never crossed my mind my action could be misinterpreted.

"Just hold it, son. Right there." It was the kind of graveled voice you didn't say "Or what?" to.

I turned toward it, halfway out the open door. A blinding flashlight beam came full into my face, and I just froze, one hand holding (still) my seat belt latch, the other on the door.

"Now, very slowly, show me both your open hands. Now, turn around and put them on your car roof. Keep them there and move your feet toward me — that's right — and spread your legs apart." The same voice said that, too. I discovered that position, leaning up against a car, made a person feel real helpless . . . open to abuse.

"Jeezum, Walt . . ." another voice began, and stopped. Heavy hands went over me, ungently: underarms, my pockets, up and down both legs.

"Okay. Stand up. Hands off the roof. Your license and your registration, please." If anything, he sounded even angrier.

By then, the second cop had gone around to the passenger side of the Subaru and was bending to look in the window. No wonder I had thought I recognized his voice; I knew the guy. I *liked* him, once had almost worshiped him. When he had been the captain of the baseball team at Dustin High, I had been a batboy at home games. His name was Jim Colangelo, and he not only hit that thing a mile but also thanked the batboy for a jacket or the weighted doughnut that he slipped onto his bat when standing in the on-deck circle. I knew most members of the town police by name, but Jim I really *knew*.

125

I'd see him and he'd say, "Hey, Gabe. Still laying off that high pitch, babe?" Different stuff like that.

I fished my wallet out, removed my license, and handed it to Sergeant Walter Armistead, the other, older cop.

I said, "I think the registration's in the glove compartment."

He said, "*I* think it better be. So get it." I bent inside the door and reached in front of Dori. Exhale; there it was. I handed it to Sergeant Armistead.

"Take them in the car and write this up," he said to Jim, holding out the stuff I'd given him.

Jim came around and took my license and the registration.

"Please come with me," he said to me. Then, looking at the sergeant, he said, "Her? Her, too?" He jerked a thumb toward Dori.

"Didn't I say 'them'?" the sergeant rasped. "Does 'them' mean one or two, to you?"

"Please come with me," Jim bent and said to Dori.

We sat in the backseat of the squad car. There were no door window handles there. I'd gotten in first and sat by the window; Dori sat so close to me our knees were touching. Jim talked to us through the metal grille that separated the front seat from the back.

"Sorry about this, Gabe," he said, looking down and writing. "But you sure did run that stop sign."

My heart had settled down by then, almost.

"I know I did," I said. "I looked for lights both ways — though that's not an excuse, I know. But Jim" — I dared to say, but softly — "since when

126

do you guys pat down people running stop signs? Wasn't that a little . . . well, *extreme?*"

"Oh, you know Walt," he said. He still did not look up at me. He'd taken off his hat when he got in the car and it had left a little crease below the hairline on his forehead, just the way his batting helmet used to.

"Well, what's he doing now?" asked Dori, suddenly. Everybody knew that Sergeant Armistead had also been a sergeant in the service — and a drill instructor, too. There was a story that he'd said if he could have the twenty biggest losers in the high school for a month at wherever he used to work, he'd guarantee to bring them back as different people, citizens that Dustin would be proud of.

"Oh, I don't know," Jim answered, vaguely, still not making any eye contact. Of course he knew, and so did Dori, so did I. He was looking for drugs in my car. Or alcohol. Or letters to the editor, perhaps. Or possibly he was *putting* something in there, to be found by him or someone else, then or later on. That, I'm sad to say, is what this kid was thinking, then.

Jim's head came up at last and looked straight at me.

"You don't have anything to worry about," he said. He looked at both of us. "Or do you?"

"No," we both said, pretty much in chorus.

"Then you don't," he said. "I promise you." It seemed as if he'd read my mind. He rolled my license and the registration up and shoved them through the grille. Then he took my ticket off his clipboard and did the same with it.

"We've got to stop meeting like this," he said to me, and smiled. "Okay?"

"Right," I said, and smiled myself. "But — one last thing." If he was going to be that nice, why not? "Don't think I'm being paranoid, but . . . how come your car was there tonight, almost opposite my house? Isn't that unusual? A squad car sitting in a quiet residential neighborhood on Thursday night at nine-eighteen P.M. . . . Oh, God." I broke it off. "I've got to pick my *mother* up" — I checked my watch — "like, *now*. Please, Jim. She's waiting at the clinic for me. Can't you. . . ?"

He knew my mother and they liked each other, too. "Sure," he said. "Hold on."

He left the car, and barely had he done so when the sergeant also scrambled out of ours. They stood beside it, talking, hat brims almost touching, and then Jim came on back and let us out.

"Just watch those stop signs, Gabe," he said, and gave me one quick wink and, like, a little nod. The sergeant didn't even look at me; he just got in the squad car, started up that throbbing, muscular V-8. I let them drive off first, then fired up my little wimpy four and tiptoed toward the clinic.

My mother hadn't had to wait that long. She listened to our explanation of what happened, saying only, "Strange." Then she turned to Dori and she asked her if instead of going home, she'd like to stay the night with us. This had happened other times, before, so I was not surprised, exactly. Just more along the lines of "awestruck," you could say. My mother had this way of sizing up a situation in half the time that it would take to tell her what the situation was. Dori said she'd love to; she'd just call her dad and let him know. When we got home, the three of us made tea and then a pan of brownies that we sampled, warm, with Granny Smith apples, while we talked about a lot of real important stuff like food, my parents' honeymoon (!) and running shoes.

When we were racking stuff inside the dishwasher, my mother said the only thing that anybody said about . . . like, *problems*.

"As far as what went on tonight. . . ." She gestured "out there," vaguely. "I think we should remember things are pretty much stirred up all over, nowadays. It's not just *here*, or *us*. A major pendulum is swinging, maybe — starting to. Toward the better, I believe. And meanwhile, lucky us" — she grinned — "we have each other."

"I'm setting my alarm for five," I told them as we headed for the stairs. "To make another pan of b's. This one for Señor Maduro."

"Good, wake me up," said Dori. "I have to study, too."

"Wake *me* up and die," my mother said.

21
MOTHERS

"But Mommy *said* . . ." I whined that at Lafountain, *obviously* kidding, right?

"Look. Gabe," Lafountain said to me. He, I knew, was trying to sound downtown, professional yupscale. "You *know* I like your mother. She's one terrific *gal*. And I buh-*lieve* 'most everything she says." He went back to his normal voice. "Especially the stuff about my manners and my clothes, compared to yours."

"Well . . . then, *what*?" I raised the haughty eyebrow.

"What you said don't fit with this new evidence I've got," Lafountain said. "I didn't even tell you yet. *My* mother just told *me*, this morning."

We were lolling in Lafountain's room, digesting. It was almost forty-eight hours since I'd gotten my first traffic ticket. That made it Saturday — and also Halloween. His mother'd fed us pot roast, gravy, noodles, salad and two slabs of apple pie (apiece) underneath (don't puke) mint-chocolate-chip ice cream. For after-dinner stimulation — instead of going to the theater or the ballet, or seducing some young actress or contessa, or trading day-old diamond mines for tropical resorts — I'd brought up my mother's optimistic thought: that maybe things were changing in our town. That possibly the pendulum was swinging — starting to, at least.

"No way," he'd said. And, slightly later on, "Get this."

It seems Lafountain's mother is a Byoutifactions client. You remember Byoutifactions, don't you? T. Hank Nevins's successful chain of hair and skin and exercise salons? Well, Mrs. L. had been at hers, the one in downtown Dustin, possibly two days before. She'd been stretching on a mat behind, and hidden from, the Firmathize machines when she had overheard two other women talking. Real excitedly, she said. They were going to *do* something, something unrelated to their hair or skin or flab. "At last," they said. And they were going to do it in the Dustin High School parking lot, starting close to nine P.M., on Saturday. During the Halloween Hop.

I hate to keep you hanging in suspense ("do it, ladies, *do* it!"), but first a word or two about this "Hop," its history and so forth.

It was a dance, of course; the first one was in 1926, the year the old part of our present school was built. Back then, the kids would all dress up like cut-outs in a grade school window (I get this info from my father; don't ask me how *he* knows). In other words, they came as ghosts and witches, skeletons and pumpkins, and black cats. When they weren't treading on each other's toes, they'd stuff their faces full of doughnuts and sweet cider, and then go bob for apples. I wouldn't be surprised if tails got pinned on donkeys, too. After, everybody'd go straight home (can you *imagine* this?) except for the town bad boys who'd do some harmless but outrageous things with mailboxes and garden gates and privies. The next day being All Saints' Day, most everyone would get up and go to seven o'clock Mass, after which a lot of adults would hear about the privies and go "tut-tut-tut" (but with "heh-heh" in their hearts). I don't blame you if you can't believe this stuff; I'm just repeating what my father said.

In any case, some decades passed and times did change (my father, *so* profoundly, added). Dustin got a dome, was not a mill town any longer. Then was then, but now is Now, and so forth.

Although the Hop is still a costume party, the standard set of characters has . . . well, been *supplemented*. People come as Klansmen, and as semi-comic Nazis; masks are very popular. You see some bands (The Beastie Boys and AC/DC), and solo stars like Billy Idol and Madonna, still, and actors and actresses and presidents, even Richard Nixon (still). It also got to be a thing to use the Hop to take revenge on people who'd been "asking for it."

Such as (last year): the girl who'd dropped the starting quarterback, causing him to get bummed-out and start to throw a lot of interceptions in the next three games. She found herself surrounded, in the girls' room, by a half a dozen "cheerleaders," all with hairy legs and Dolly Parton masks. They carefully undressed her, altogether, put a football helmet on her head, and shoved her out the girls' room door. Then they wedged the door shut and (presumably) jumped out the window. She, meanwhile, ran up behind a "ghost" and tore the sheet right off its back, revealing Mr. Kriendler (physics) in just a gappy, one-piece union suit, and Hush Puppies.

Such as, again (from the year before that): Two "Ronald Reagans" beat the shit out of a "Boy George," right behind the soda booth.

I'm sure you get the picture, or the trend — whatever.

But it wasn't anything about the costumes or the "pranks" that bothered those two women that Lafountain's mother overheard. They had something else in mind to "do." Their plan was to crack down on post-Hop drinking. Thud.

The *modus operandi* they were going to use was really simple. While the Hop was hopping, still, these high school mothers and their friends were going to search their children's schoolmates' *cars*. They'd do this from the outside, using flashlights. That meant that they were "legal" and could get "police cooperation" (so Lafountain's mother heard them say). If they saw a "beverage" inside a car, they'd take the license number down. And when its driver tried to leave the lot, the cops would pull him over. The rule that said no one could leave the Hop until it ended made the mothers' work much easier. And their kids — that is to say those *other* people's kids — would plain go nuts trying to figure out how the cops *knew*, just from looking at their cars.

Those mothers that Lafountain's mother overheard — they "couldn't wait" for Saturday.

"Assuming that you're right — your mother's right, I mean," I babbled at Lafountain, me now bouncing up and down excitedly on his spare bed, "or even if she isn't, we should check it out, the parking lot, I mean. I can't believe this, really. Except of course I can. It's just so typical. I wonder whose idea it was, originally. It stinks of Leeds, no kidding. An' you know what? I feel another *letter* coming on!"

"Whoa!" Lafountain said. "Kid Gabe here's strapping on his trusty old . . . *thesaurus* — is it? Will he drop some sentence fragments on them snoopy broads, or what? He could maim a mom for life, no shit."

I'd gotten up by then, was heading for the door.

"Hold on. Before we go . . ." Lafountain said. He had that geeky look he gets when he believes he's on a roll.

"Well . . . *what?*" I asked the guy, again.

"I'm just not sure we're *ready* yet," Lafountain said, "to face — no, wait, I'm serious — a bunch of other people's *mothers*. Shouldn't we, like. . . ." He rose and pantomimed a cowpoke pushing those two swinging doors apart and walking into an old wild West saloon. He went a few steps farther, then he leaned an elbow on the bar and pushed his hat back on his head. "*Scope*," he grated, hoarsely. "Leave the bottle."

134

I moaned and pushed the joker out the bedroom door ahead of me. And so we left the house, hearts beating wildly, our breath still smelling faintly of mint-chocolate-chip, I'm sure.

We parked a safe three blocks away, and so approached the high school parking lot on foot, and from its darkest side. Thanks to the widely scattered floodlights in the lot, it was a cinch to spot our quarry, right away. There were eight of them in all, split up in groups of four. Even from a distance they looked dangerous: mostly chunky women, wearing pants and (oddly) in the case of five of them, those *sun visors* that female golfers pile their hair on top of, both on the women's tour and at the local links, The Golden Swing C.C. But, instead of scorecards, some of these had clipboards in their hands.

"We've got to get up close," I whispered to Lafountain. "I want to hear exactly what they say."

He nodded. "Yeah," he said. "And maybe we can recognize a couple. Wouldn't that be great?"

"I guess," I said. In certain ways, I didn't want to know. It's likely I felt sorry for their kids, already.

Bent way over, ducking down between the rows of cars, we headed for the middle of the lot. I figured we could slide beneath a pair of cars the moms had searched already. And then just let them come to us, one of those two groups of four. I chose an old Bellair sedan; Lafountain had the new Dodge pickup right beside it. Across the empty aisle in front of us, there was a Tercel wagon and a Subaru GT. The mothers were perhaps, oh, twenty cars away.

As they approached, fragments of their sentences, their *style*, preceded them.

135

" . . . she doesn't give a sweet *petite*. Why this one time she told me I should. . . ."

" . . . toss them right the hell in jail. . . . I know, I know, but still. You tell me how. . . ."

I could see their feet and lower legs by then. Two pairs of Nikes, one New Balance, one $6.99 at 3-D Discount. They had reached the Subaru.

"Oh, I think I know whose *this* one is." I'll call the speaker mother number one. "That Gabriel Pateski. Or 'Protesto,' as my husband says."

Clunk. I hadn't been prepared for that. Fame. Celebrity. Mistaken car identity.

"Or whatever," number two agreed, or seemed to, anyway. Now I wished that I could see their faces.

"He's in Eddie's homeroom," number two went on. EddieEddieEddie. There was only one. This must be Mrs. Gratz. "Eddie says he's not too bad a kid" — oh, thank you, Eddie dearest — "but as far as I'm concerned, he's gotten way too big for his blue denim britches."

"Fred says if he was ours, he'd kick his ass but good," said number one. "What's the matter with his *parents*, anyway?"

"The father isn't home that much, I heard," said number three. "I think he's got something to do with professional sports. I hear he comes and goes a lot."

"I bet," said number one, and snickered. "I *bet* he does. Fred told me all the different sports have their own groupies, nowadays. I told him that I bet he'd like a job like that, banging redheads coast to coast. He said not with that AIDS he wouldn't. I *still* think it's a blessing in disguise."

136

"Well, I don't see a thing in there," a new voice said. That made her number four. The New Balances moved off, toward the Tercel.

"No, wait," said number one, "I'd really like to nail Pateski, here. You know his mother runs that clinic downtown, don't you? My daughter's girlfriend said they tell the girls to carry birth control on dates, can you believe it?" I saw the front door of the Subaru fly open.

"Hey, Jeanine," said number two, "you know the sergeant said we can't do that. No searching, like, without a warrant."

"What's the diff?" said number one. But I could tell she wasn't in the car yet. "I don't see why it's all that big a deal. The law says kids this age can't have the stuff, so all we're doing, either way, is helping to enforce a law. Alcohol is all that interests me. If someone left a pile of hundred dollar bills just sitting in the glove compartment . . . hey, I wouldn't even touch 'em. You know, I'm not so sure a kid Pateski's age has any legal rights at all. I mean, he's just a minor."

She went up on one toe, and one foot disappeared — as if she'd put a knee, like, on a car seat. But pretty soon she once again was firmly planted on the ground.

"Damn!" she said. "There isn't anything in there but these. I got half a mind to stick a pin in them. Serve the little faggot right."

"Cut it out, Jeanine," said number four. "That isn't funny. Think about the girl, why don't you?"

I would have given anything to see. Could she have found some condoms in the car? It sounded very much as if she had — which wouldn't be surprising to her, if she thought the car was mine.

"I was only kidding." Number one, her shoes, stepped back; the Subaru's front door slammed shut, and I mean *slammed*. Somebody went "Shh"; the feet all circled the Tercel.

"Hey, look," said number one, but in a whisper, this time. "Underneath the paper bag. How's that song go on TV? 'Da-da da da da the Silver Bullet to*ni-ight*.' . . !" And everybody giggled. That Jeanine.

To this day, I claim it was a rat. Lafountain says he *saw* it, and it was a *cat* — a black and white one. Here is what I know for sure: Some quick and furry *something* romped across the back parts of my knees and thighs, and I came out from under that Bellair as quickly as a service station guy who's heard the coffee truck pull in. Lafountain, maybe thinking I'd decided to attack, came dutifully after.

No suitable quotations popped into my mind, I'm sad to say. ("Lafountain, we are here" would not have worked at all, in case you thought of that one as a possibility.) *Surprise* was on my side, however.

"Good evening, ladies," I said smoothly, as the rapid beating of my rat-scared heart abated slightly. "Lose something, perhaps?"

They gaped and gawked at me. Having teenaged sons or daughters must prepare a mother for a lot of things. Most probably, she's earned the right to have a "Shock Resistant" on her label. But still, boys-popping-out-from-under-cars was nowhere on these mothers' program. Not just then, or there. And especially, as mother three (?) now gasped, not:

138

"Gabriel Podesta!"

"Precisely and in person, at your service," I riposted, smoothly. I could almost *feel* a rakish, thin mustache erupting on my upper lip, the kind you see in late, late movies on the face of Mr. Errol Flynn — or Gable, C. I wished I had a long black cloak on, the kind I could have swirled.

There was an instant there, I swear, when all the mothers looked like guilty little kids. But mother one (I *knew* that it was she) fought off the feeling first; her shifty, awkward eyes became defiant.

"And what do you suppose *you're* doing here?" She shrilled the words at me, at us. It was not the sort of line, or tone, that people used addressing Douglas Fairbanks, Jr. — except for maybe Queen Elizabeth the First.

"Just passing through. This is public property," I said. "A better question is what *you* are do — "

"You're meant to be *inside*," this mother shouted in my face. I got the feeling she had interrupted sixteen-year-old kids before. "You're not *allowed* to be out here until the dance is over."

Obviously, she hadn't yet admitted to her mind the possibility that there were boys and girls in town who, unlike her son or daughter, had chosen not to hop, this Halloween. Dori Fabb, in fact, had gone so far as to head out of town; she'd planned a weekend camping with two girlfriends.

"Jeanine," said mother four (?), "not all the kids in school bought tickets, by a long shot. Wendy said — "

"You don't have the authority to search the cars out here," I said. "Most of these belong to parents or to teachers." Historically, I'd done some interrupting of my own. "Two wrongs don't make a right," I said, "they never do. Your ends don't justify your means. Not even close."

As soon as that last group of sentences had left my mouth, I knew I'd scored. It was as if the Muse of Argument had come and whispered in my ear: "This one's for you, Podesta, G."

"Two wrongs don't make a right" was straight out of the Mothers' Favorite Phrases book. For these four moms, here, hearing it from me was comparable to how President Truman would have felt if the Enola Gay had taken off the week after hitting Hiroshima and dropped another Big Boy on D.C. Telling them that their ends didn't justify their means was also good, but not *as* good. It takes most people a few ticks to figure which are ends and which are means, exactly, and hence what that whole *phrase* means. As cliches go, it's just a little upscale for the Favorite Phrases book.

Anyway. Having been hit with that kind of tonnage, the mothers needed time to get their act together and assess the damage — maybe take evasive action. Mother two decided that a smokescreen mightn't hurt.

"Trevor Lafountain!" she blared out, taking one full step toward my buddy. "I *thought* that it was you. Why on earth are *you* here, Trevor?"

Probably that mother (Eddie's — Mrs. Gratz) didn't even know she'd sent up more than smoke. But "Trevor" is a missile, to Lafountain — as it is to all his friends. No one, other than his parents, calls him that; the name just isn't him. You don't call a dog house "The Fontainebleu." Nothing against Lafountain, you just don't. I expected he would throttle her, go right for the throat.

"I'm with G-Gabe," Lafountain stammered, fighting for control. Then he got his act, such as it is, together. "The two of us was passing by, and we just happened to observe what you are doing. It seemed to call for some . . . investigative action on our parts." Loyal guy; he didn't implicate his mother.

"Well. That means that's not your car, then," said mother one to me, jerking one sharp thumb toward the Subaru.

"No, indeedy," I replied. "*I* don't keep condoms in my glove compartment. I'm pretty sure that's Hobie Lowell's car. The one his father lets him use, sometimes."

Fact is, I had no idea whose Subaru that was, nor was I positive of mother one's identity. "Jeanine" had rung the faintest bell, however. It seemed to me that Jeri Puckett's mother might have been "Jeanine." And Jeri "went" with Hobie Lowell.

I couldn't see if mother one had blanched or not; the parking lot was just too dim for that. I also couldn't see the point of our prolonging this; by skill (and great good luck) we'd scored in almost every way we could. Every way but one that I'd just thought of. I turned toward Lafountain.

"What say we head on home now, hoss?" I asked the guy. "I think I'll call up Mr. Jerry Koch and ask him should we tell the town police about these ladies, here." I swiveled toward the mothers. "It isn't that I want to get you into any *trouble*," I insisted. "I

141

won't be naming any *names*, or anything. It's just that I don't think a thing like this should happen, here in Dustin."

"This isn't what our town is all *about*," Lafountain added, primly.

We made a stately exit, leaving sputtering behind.

22
DEAR GOVERNOR (2)

Dear Governor,

Yes, it's me again. This is just in case there's a misunderstanding, here.

I *know* that alcohol's a problem, especially combined with driving cars. Drinking-driving sucks, whoever's doing it. People *die*, are *killed* — including total innocents, like you-know-who.

But give me a break. That's not the point here, and I'm sure you know it.

Respectfully and sincerely,
Gabriel Podesta, Junior Class

P.S. If I ever have the chance, I'll vote for you for President, I think. And I'm not just saying that so you'll agree with me.

23
TESTS

"I couldn't possibly have AIDS," Lafountain said.

It was a lovely day beneath the dome, and the three of us were strolling back from downtown, toward the high school. November third, and we were all in shirtsleeves.

"Sure you could," said Arby Fremont. He started holding fingers up, ones on the hand that wasn't wrapped around the double peach melba ice-cream cone. He'd decided on "The Flavor of the Fortnight." "One, your mother could have passed it on to you when you were born. Nothing against your mother, but she could have got the virus accidentally — before they even *knew* about it, right?"

Lafountain shook his head. "Not *my* mother. My mother ain't the type. In fact, I'd say that if there's anyone in the whole United States that would *never* contract a disease like AIDS, it's my mother. You can ask Gabe — he knows her."

"Check," I said. My lips were glossed with chocolate swirl. I licked them off and added, "Fontsie's mother won't even take a telephone poll if the guy sounds the least bit effeminate. She wouldn't swim in the same pool with David Crosby, never. I *know* that."

"Get out," Lafountain said. And then to Arby. "He's just kidding. What she is is too *conservative*. AIDS is still too new for her. She'd wait till almost everybody had it. Or it came on sale."

"Okay, well then" — Arby held another finger up — "you might have gotten it because some nurse was feeling lazy when you had to get a shot. When you were just a kid. Maybe she didn't want to walk down to the storeroom and get a fresh box, so she just used a needle over, that one time — and the kid she did before you had it. Or" — another finger rose — "for all I know you used to get in limousines with older men with monocles. Just for pocket money, not because you liked it, naturally. *Un*-naturally, I mean." He grinned and took a big slurp on his cone.

"In fact," he said, "the only place I'm sure you didn't get the virus from is a beautiful woman. That being only because no beautiful woman would even give the time of day to a doofus like you. Of course" — he smiled his lofty smile — "they're not a high-risk group, thank God. And luckily for *me*."

"Oh, sure," I said. "Listen to the king of hearts."

If Arby was the killer Arby liked to say he was, he wouldn't have the strength to stand, most days. I turned toward Lafountain.

"Remember last year, when a certain sandwich-shop chain was thinking of locating around here? And then they did this survey and discovered when they said that one word, 'Arby,' to any nubile female in the downtown Dustin area, and asked them what it made them think of, eighty-four percent said 'dog meat'? They couldn't figure it out. Everywhere else, they got 'roast beef.' That's why they put the shop in Ellington, I heard."

"That figures," said Lafountain, nodding solemnly. "I don't blame them."

"Hey — how *could* you?" I agreed.

"You *guys* . . ." said Arby, cheerfully.

We were coming back, of course, from Iggy's Cream Dreams, Dustin's leading ice-cream boutique. It had the marble-top counter and small round tables with those small, uncomfortable wire-backed chairs. My father said that it was "pure nostalgia — a reprise of the 1930s." I asked him how he knew, him having been, like, minus eight in 1939, but he just passed it off by saying something vague about me "getting plugged-in to our common heritage."

All three of us were blessed with a free period right after lunch that day, which is why it was possible for Iggy's cones to edge out the cafeteria's yellow Jello squares as our dessert choice. And we were talking AIDS because there'd been a new development about it just that week. Not either of the ones that everybody hoped for: the vaccination or the cure, but something sort of interesting — even good. A team of people from the Center for Disease Control was coming to our school to give free AIDS tests to anyone who wanted one. Apparently, this was something they were starting to *do*, go around to schools, and the deal was that there'd be absolute confidentiality with no one *at* the school involved, and a guarantee that the results would never appear on anyone's medical records. The only reason I believe that last part is I'd asked my mother. She'd said absolutely yes, that that was how those people did it.

"They're smart," she'd said. "They want to get the high-risk people, too." She grinned. "Not just you uncurved arrows. And they know those folks are wary. As they should be."

My mother was just kidding with that arrows line, but not about some people's tendency to be extremely dubious about the test. People who were known to have the virus had been treated pretty much like lepers used to be, at different times, in different places. Kept out of jobs and housing — that. For just no reason in the world, except for the big F, as found in *Fear*.

It still freaked me out to think about AIDS. I'd been tested for the thing, already. No one knew that but Dori and my parents, I don't think — and my family physician, of course. The reason was that I'd been given blood after I'd had my tonsils out. I guess that happens with that operation, sometimes; you can lose a lot of blood. That was before they'd tested all blood donors' blood for AIDS; nowadays: No problem. So I'd had the test and it was negative, but still I didn't get AIDS off my mind. I couldn't get over the fact that, unlike all the other plagues in history, *you* had to put *yourself* at risk to get it. Except in the case of babies — and even with them, the mother could find out if she was liable to give it. In other words, people had a choice. Whether they'd get it and, if they had it, whether they'd give it. You'd think those facts'd make this dumb disease real easy to control, but no. When we are playing games of "dumb," we human beings have to give the opposition points.

"So, you're not going to take the test, are you?" Arby said to me. (I give you one example, right away.) "I'm not."

"*Sure* I am," I said to him. "I conceivably could have the virus."

"What?" Lafountain said. "And *now* he tells me!"

"Gosh, I'm sorry, dear," I said. And then I told them both about my tonsillectomy and having the transfusion, afterwards. I didn't say that I had had the test already, though. Of course not.

"Well, *I* never got a transfusion," Arby said. "My blood's pure Fremont-Miles. High octane and a hundred proof. That's my mother's side, the Mileses."

"Yeah — *but*," Lafountain said, sarcastically. "You Casanovas are a pretty high-risk group, you know. Even if you never did it with a girl who did it with a bi- — oh, back when you were eight or nine, let's say, before all this began, when you were — let's be delicate — too *young* to use a condom, even — there's always, well, the kissing possibility."

"You can't get AIDS from kissing, that's a lot of

148

bull," said Arby promptly. A little *too* promptly.

"We-ell," Lafountain said. "You *probably* can't. But I asked Gabe's mother — she *knows* this kind of stuff. I put it to her straight: How about French kissing? You see, that's sort of like a *specialité* of mine. A lot of girls — "

"Cut the shit," said Arby. "What'd she say?"

"She said there *was* a real small possibility," Lafountain smirked, and nodded. "That if you kissed a girl who had the virus — it *has* shown up, but rarely, in saliva — and you had like a cut inside your mouth. Let's say that you just bit your tongue. Or maybe she had. Then you *could* pick up the virus from her."

Arby turned to me. "Is this guy telling me the truth? I bite my tongue a lot. Well, not my tongue, exactly — more like this one place on the inside of my lower lip, here." He moved his tongue around in there. "Like, where you've got a little *bump*, like. . . ?"

"He's right," I told him. "As he said, it's real remote, the possibility. But it exists, I guess."

"Boy," said Arby. "I'm gonna tell a lot of *chicks* to take the test, for sure. That'd really *suck* — getting it from, like, a girl, that way."

By then, we'd gotten real close to the school. We left the street, as usual, to cut on through the city playground next to it. That was where the Wonkers tended to hang out, in this one corner of the playground, in the early afternoon, when the grade school kids were still in school. Basically, they were a bunch of kids who weren't much involved with school. They came more as a social thing, the ones who did. Even the ones who'd actually dropped *out* dropped by the playground, though. Some of them got high a lot, some of them were burnouts. Some just hung around. I thought they seemed real bored most of the time. That day, there were about a dozen of them there, sitting on the seesaws, lying on the slides, leaning up against the jungle gym. I threw some hi's at four or five I knew, one of whom got up and came toward us.

"Hey, Gabe," he said. "Talk to you a minute, man?"

The kid was William Schluter, better known as "Straight." He was a fairly famous member of our class, I'd say. What he also was was totally fanatical about the sixties, the Beats, the early hippies, and the flower children, peace and love — all that. *On the Road* — he'd almost memorized that book. I thought he was a lot like a movie character, almost a cliché: you know, the really gifted nonconformist, the one that everybody *knows* will get to be real famous, if he doesn't die in some romantic, stupid, wasteful way. He was even good at Art and English, for Pete's sake.

Arby and Lafountain also stopped when I did.

"Sure," I said to William. "What's happening, your Straight-ness?"

"Look," he said to Arby and Lafountain. "I don't see no sense in trying to make some kind of goofbang deal of this. The plain unvarnished is: I want to talk to Gabe alone."

"*Well*," Lafountain said, huffy as they come. "I'd never speak for Arbuthnot, but me, I wouldn't stay a sec where I'm not wanted, Willie. And anyways, I'm not so sure that being seen with you is what I'd like to have recorded on my . . . record."

Making one big show of it, he glanced up toward the corner of the second floor of the high school, where the principal's office was. Arby couldn't help but do the same, which made the other three of us all point at him and laugh.

"Screw you guys," he said, and started off.

"Hey, Arbs," Lafountain said. "Wait up." He hustled after him and put a hand up on his shoulder. "I really think I saw him watching, honest Injun. . . ."

"Gabe," Straight Schluter said, "you're in the pipeline, here. So take me on your knee and let the level truth abound. What kind of sordid business is this AIDS test, anyway?"

"Well," I said, "they're going to have it in — "

" — the gym, I know," he said. "That gives me sweats of joy to start with. And if your last name starts with Tweedle-dee or -dum, you got to go at such-and-such a time. I dig. In the case of you and me, that time is two P.M. But that's not what I'm after, the mechanicals. I want to penetrate the marrow of the thing. *Could* this be some buffle-headed scheme for getting all the gays and shooters into freight cars? Knowing that these guys are Feds in no way fills my heart with major gladness, I can tell you that. These maniacs" — he jerked his thumb back at the other Wonkers — "are pondering the question: Suppose they take the test and don't do good on it? Will their little rumble seats end up in Idaho?"

"I've gotta think there's Feds and Feds," I said. "My mother said if we can't trust these people, then the country's got a problem."

"Tell me about it," William said, and laughed.

"So maybe what I need to hear," he said "is if a lot of kids like you are taking it."

"Like *me*?" I said. I laid an open hand right on my heart, the way that Opus does. "Of *course* not. When did you *ever* see another kid with my complexity and depth, my looks and personality, my purity and perspicaci — "

"All *right*," said William. "Then how about we just say *un*like me?"

"I don't know. I'm trying to talk it up," I said. "*I* think everybody ought to take the thing, don't you?"

"Yeah," he said. "I do. Perhaps I've lost what little sense I ever had but — well — I almost *have to*, is the truth of it. I'd be the foulest hypocrite on earth if I infected some sweet innocent, by accident or ignorance." He smiled and twisted one long lock of hair around his index finger. "How could I come down on Reagan, if I did a thing like that?"

"You wouldn't want to give up politics," I said. "I can understand that, Straight."

"Well, see you in the lineup, then, I guess," he said.

"We'll get by with a little help from our friends," I told him.

" ' . . . from our friends,' " he echoed, as he turned away. " 'And don't you know that God is Pooh Bear?' "

The last of that I recognized as being straight from Kerouac, of course.

152

* * *

That night, I talked to Dori on the phone. She said that she'd been talking up the test all day. Apparently, a lot of girls had just decided they would take it, for their own good reasons. Some of them had slept around enough to be afraid they could have picked the virus up, one time or another. Others wanted to have proof that they could show a boyfriend (present or potential), or their mothers. Still other ones, like D herself, were doing it to keep friends company — to produce the sort of crowd scene William had been hoping for. (Girls *are* more together, naturally — I keep noticing that fact.) The few who weren't going to take it, Dori said, were mostly ones who thought (or anyway, they *said*) that AIDS was sent by God to punish evildoers. "Not that everybody doesn't know their names, already."

Dori, being Fabb, was in the A to F's, at ten A.M.

She found me in the late lunch line, at one.

"Come here," she grabbed my arm, began to tug on it. "I've got to talk to you." Her idea (obviously) was for me to leave my place in line. And it was taco day.

"Wait. Hold on. I've got to eat," I said. "I'm starving."

"Shut up. I've got a half a sandwich you can have," she said, pulling me along, me giving in. "I told you it's important. It's about the test." Then I went fast and quietly.

We bounded out the main front door and on around the side where there were steps that went up to another door you couldn't open from outside.

153

She handed me a half a tuna salad, hold the mayo, on some curling whole wheat bread.

"Let me ask you something," Dori said. "The test — it gives false-positive results, sometimes?"

So that was it. "Yeah," I said, already chewing. "Yeah, I've heard that's right. A certain small percentage always gets false-positive. Like you probably just did, right? Well, look. Don't — "

But she was saying, "No, that isn't it. They're not set up to screen your blood right on the spot, you idiot. What happened is, they've got this other test. Part Two, they called it. After they took the sample, you walked out the far door, and girls went to the girls' locker room and boys to the boys'. *Then* they got another sample, for this backup test, they said."

"What? What backup test? Another sample? Where'd they get it from, your other arm?"

"No," she said. "This one was a urine sample. They said it could be used — your urine could be used — to double-check your blood, in case you got a positive. They said the virus is in urine, too. I think I *saw* that, in Ann Landers. And I'll tell you something else: They sure were super-careful, getting it."

"I bet," I said. Of course. But check it out. "How do you mean, exactly?"

Dori dropped her eyes. "They had, like, *proctors* in the girls' room. It was pretty embarrassing. Brautigan was one of them. They only used every other stall and you had to keep the door open. I guess so's you couldn't get, like, someone else to do your sample for you. Though why anyone would want . . .

154

What? What's all *that* for, anyway?" I was giving her some major head-shakes: contradictory and negative. "You don't think that was the reason?"

"I think it was the *reason*," I replied. "But I don't think that was an AIDS test. First of all, my mother said she was sure they wouldn't let any of the school personnel have anything to do with the testing. Plus, I just don't think there *is* a urine test for AIDS. But remember in the *Dustin Times*, that editorial? I bet you A to F's all took a drug test. And, by now, the G to L's have, too."

"No!" said Dori. "Shit! You know, I actually *wondered* about that. But then I thought they wouldn't dare. Not unless they told us first. Some kids are going to want to *kill* me!"

"Did everybody do it? Far as you could tell?"

"I *think*," she said. "I heard they made the ones who *couldn't*, wait. It all seemed on the up-and-up. Except for Brautigan, I'd never seen the people. You gave your little bottle to this nurse. It only had your number on it."

"But Brautigan could see who handed in what number, right?"

"I guess," she shrugged. "I pretty much avoided looking at her, if you want to know the truth."

"Well, I said, "it sounds like just about the perfect scam. People take a voluntary AIDS test, given by these outside people. Then they're made to think the test has got another part. So, *voluntarily*, they leave a urine sample, except this time, unbeknownst to them, they hand it to a *different* group of outside people who are working for the school, instead of for the government."

Dori stared at me.

"Well, maybe we can get our samples *back*," she said. "I bet that they're still there. And meanwhile, you — *You* aren't going to give a urine sample, are you?"

"Heavens *no*," I said. "Let Leeds keep thinking I'm a junkie. Look. I ought to go. But here's what we can do." I'd gotten this idea, a really novel one: Call out the cavalry. "You go down to the pay phone on the corner. Get my mother at the clinic. Tell her the whole story. Maybe I'm completely nuts. Possibly there *is* a backup urine test for AIDS: She'll know. But tell her I'm not going to take it — and . . . and that I'm going to make a scene about it, and not take it. That's unless . . . unless she gets a message to me, *somehow*, that I should." I laughed. "She'll have to figure out how. Okay? That may not be the best scenario, but it's all that I can think of. See, what I want is everybody taking that first blood test, and then — "

"Okay," said Dori, interrupting. "Sure. Just tell me what the clinic's number is. . . ." I did so.

"Okay," she said again. "I'm off. And, Gabe. . . ?"

"Yes . . . what?" I said.

"Well, keep your powder dry," she said. *Absurdly*, if I heard her right.

The taking of the blood was pretty competently done, I thought. I have *so* much to compare it with, of course: all the other times I've stood around for just that purpose with possibly a hundred kids my age, half of whom are slightly spooked by what's about to happen, but are trying not to show it.

156

I base that last estimate on my own feelings, naturally, and on the *super* job I did on their disguise.

"Who heard how much they're gonna take?" I babbled.

"Erin said it's, like, a half a test tube full, she thought," said Allison Margolis.

"That much?" said Chris Polander. "Why do they need so much, just to do one test? I thought they'd maybe prick your finger, smear it on a slide, like in biology."

"No way," said Allison. "I heard what they're checking out is not the virus but, like, antibodies in your blood. Whatever they are."

"Betcha Gabe has lotsa *them*," said Big John Rocca. "Guy with a built like him." Big John looked pleased — *delighted* — with his subtle verbal humor. Big John laughed. "Body like he's got, he ain't got more'n one or two *pro*-bodies, I can tell you that much." Big John laughed again and looked around, making sure that everyone had got it. Two or three real toadies smiled tight smiles and nodded. I went, "Sure-sure-sure, Big John."

"What Sheila said," said Allison, "was one guy passed right out, from looking at his blood come out." She giggled. "Just imagine that. She didn't want to tell me who it was; I hadda worm it out of her. You wouldn't guess it in a million years. I mean, you wouldn't think a guy like . . . well, I shouldn't say, I guess. . . ." She laughed again and rolled her eyes around.

There were five or six people, all in white, who were actually doing the bloodletting. All of them were women, I was glad to see. It just struck me

157

that women would be more competent and careful, taking blood. That's possibly a sexist thought, but I can't help it. To me, it feels more like a compliment.

I hadn't made any particular effort to be one of the first ones in line. Actually, I wanted to give my mother as much time as possible to stop me from making a scene, if that was what it all came down to. I remember seeing old newsreels, going back to the days of Prohibition, of treasury agents pouring these confiscated bottles of bootleg gin and whiskey down in to a storm sewer some place. That seemed a little more glamorous, somehow, than standing over a toilet emptying a bunch of little things of piss. Maybe that's a liquidist remark, but I can't help *it*, either.

When my turn came to give the blood . . . say- hey, it was a breeze! No sweat, no problem, none at all. Well, maybe a *little* sweat, just coursing down my ribs as I sat down. The woman wrapped this length of rubber tube around my arm; I hardly felt the pinprick of the needle. Drawing out the blood took hardly any time (well, no, I *didn't* watch), and the next thing I knew I was holding this little piece of gauze inside my up-bent arm and it was over.

As Dori'd said, we had to leave the gym through either the boys' or the girls' locker room, depending. And just inside that door was a person handing you a little bottle and saying (just as Dori'd said) that this was Part Two of the test, and stuff about "a backup" and "false-positives." The person was a guy, in our case, in the kind of all-white suit and shoes that makes you think of labs and hospitals.

And in the bathroom, big as life (but on the scrawny side, as usual) was Dr. Leeds. He also had a clean white jacket on, his stethoscope just peeking out of a side pocket. He was looking like the host of some big party, wreathed in smiles.

"Every other urinal," he said. I thought he took care not to catch my eye.

I took my stance but never touched the zipper. My sort-of plan was just to stand there with my back to him and to the other white suits, one of whom was seated in a chair behind a table, with a lot of rows of samples all lined up, already — and some cases with more samples at his feet. Eventually, they'd notice me, just standing there, and *someone* would say *something*. Then, I'd decided to reply as follows:

"I refuse to cooperate with this test on the basis of the Fourth Amendment of the United States Constitution."

I figured that'd be a stunner. *You* know and *I* know that Article IV of the Bill of Rights says: "The right of the people *to be secure in their persons*, houses, papers and effects *against unreasonable searches and seizures*, shall not be violated, and no warrants shall issue but upon probable cause, supported by oath or affirmation, and *particularly describing the place to be searched*, and the persons or *things to be seized*." (Italics mine.) But how many people who habitually wear white coats have any idea what the Fourth Amendment says? I imagined lots of "What's-all-this"-ing, to which I'd keep on saying that one sentence —

159

while a crowd of new arrivals, clutching empty bottles, tried to figure out just what the hell was going
on.

But as so often happens in my life, the real event
was far, far different than the one I'd planned on.
Before my statue act attracted any notice, I (we-
everyone) heard voices raised out in the locker room.
And soon their owners were a doorful of extremely
angry-looking, overheated men, all dressed in power
suits and sports coats.

They flowed into the white-tiled space, many of
them talking simultaneously, but saying lots of different things, all negative.

"This is the biggest goddam *outrage*, yet!" That
shouter was none other than Llewellyn Fabb.
Though in the second row of men, he was looking
to push through the bodies massed in front of him.
Based on the movements he was making with his
hands and arms, I would, if we'd been teammates
in charades, have guessed that he was doing "Tear
them limb from limb."

"Please." Mr. Jerry Koch's familiar voice rose over
all the rest. "Dr. Leeds. We've reason to believe
what's taking place here is a collection of some Dustin High School students' urine for a drug test. If
true, these actions run directly counter, we believe,
to the State Board of Education's directive concerning general drug testing, and promulgated in a letter
sent to all the local school boards in October of last
year. Here with me, as you have no doubt noticed,
are the fathers of a number of these students. Students' mothers, to an even greater number, are at
this moment in the girls' room. We demand that this

collection cease at once, that all these urine samples be disposed of, and that the personnel of" — he spoke in an undertone to one of the white-clad men — "Acme Screening Labs be told the town of Dustin has no further need for any of their services, beyond disposal."

The men standing behind and around Mr. Koch then raised their voices once again, in strong agreement, this time. Then other messages rang out. Mr. Fabb was shouting, "Get those Hessians out of here! Impeach the school directors!" I realized many of the other men were local heavyweights. I recognized a former school director, a state senator (who was also senior partner in a major downtown law firm), the owner of the restaurant, Piccanteria, and some others. And, in the distant background of the group, not quite a part of it but making not the slightest try to get to Leeds's side, one T. Hank Nevins.

Leeds tried to babble things about a "strictly voluntary" test, and how that fell within the state department's guidelines, but it didn't wash. He said he'd take the matter up with "counsel for the school," but he supposed that in the meantime they should " . . . well, *abort* this test." He spoke to three white-suited guys, and each of them took cases of the urine samples to the toilets and began to empty them, one bottle at a time.

I started to applaud, and pretty soon the noise in there was pretty close to deafening — yeah, lots of piercing whistles and the chant of "Flush-flush-flush-flush-flush-flush-flush," as kids came crowding in, both from the gym and from the halls.

My mother later told me that we'd had some luck,

at her end of the deal. Dori's call had just happened to come during a meeting of the board of directors of the clinic, which meant she had a lot of sympathetic help right there. Each of them could think of friends to call, and all of them were ready to head down to school with her. And one of them — Mr. Jerry Koch, of course — just happened to have recently checked out state policy on drug tests in the public schools, and had that information in his briefcase. Sometimes you get the breaks, I guess.

The next time I saw William Schluter, he yelled, "Gabe! Some goofbang kind of show, man!" And shook his head, and laughed.

24
LIBRARY CARDS

In towns the age and size of Dustin, the public library is apt to have a female name. No doubt I learned that from my father, the historian. It was almost surely he who told me that the wife of probably the richest man in town, the one who'd made his fortune five times over even as he kept on paying coolie wages to the workers in his mills, would decide that she'd do something nice for *all* the people in the town, including those poor workers in the mills, *their* wives and families. Sometimes the something nice would be a hospital. Everyone can use a hospital. *Everyone* gets sick and dies. Other times she'd give a public library. Not everyone has time, or taste, for reading. But that she couldn't help. Everyone who *wanted to* could use a public library.

In Dustin's case, the library was given by, and

therefore took the name of, Mabel Archer Winston. The Archers dropped one place, to second richest family in town, after Mabel married Norris Winston and her parents died and left her half their money. You can guess who took the Archers place atop the charts. Nowadays, the Winstons and the Archers, both, are only upper-average. Once their mills got sick and closed, they had to send out resumés and interview for jobs, like everybody else.

Two Saturdays after Halloween, I got up in the morning with a great idea; it shimmered in the forefront of my brain. The day before, it had arrived in ordinary clothes, but over time I'd talked it into gold lamé — not too hard a job at all. As ideas go, it really did look great, to me. Get this: I'd go down to the Mabel Archer Winston Library, in town, and talk to Mr. Fabb. That very day, that Saturday. Ta-da!

Two reasons for this expedition, both of them darn good. First, I wanted to evaluate the guy, my-self — to see exactly how far gone he was. I had, I felt, to do that well away from Dori *and* his kitchen table. That kitchen table was his space-place, I'd decided. I'd seen him at it three times since the night she'd told me he was popping pills while also drinking alcohol, the hard stuff. On each of those occasions he'd looked spacey, bombed. But (I had to ask myself) wasn't that the way he'd *always* looked, when he was sitting there? Dori'd said she wasn't sure, herself, just what-all he was doing in the way of drugs and alcohol. She'd said there wasn't any vodka underneath the kitchen sink, or anywhere else where she could find it. But she also thought he'd lately looked a little worse, more wasted. What did I think, honestly? (she asked). I said he seemed about the same. Now I could take a longer look, on neutral ground.

My second reason was to see if maybe I could steer him to the clinic. That'd be regardless of my judgment on his present state of mind. Addict or no addict (alcoholic, possibly) the guy could use some counseling. *But* — he'd have to choose to get it. I'd read about these kids who turned their parents in for drug use. That doesn't seem to me to be the proper way to go — unless a person has to do it for his own protection. I've read the Nazis used to train young kids to check on their own parents, and to turn them in for this-and-that. I'm not sure I'd ever want the government to lock up in a cell and treat — "reform" — a member of my family. What I hoped to do was sort of jolly Mr. Fabb along, say that maybe things were not *that* bad in town, bring up my mother's pendulum idea. Perhaps he'd like to talk with *her* about it, I'd suggest — it and any other stuff he thought was relevant to all our situations.

So, wasn't I both devious and subtle, quite the little master-planner, junior-mental-health-professional? Hope to kiss a pig (as Uncle Snuffy says).

The day before, I'd laid this out for Dori — all I hoped to do — and asked for her opinion. She'd looked at me and said, "Good *luck*." The tone and emphasis she gave the second word suggested she had not been sucked into the vortex of my hopefulness.

But still, that Saturday, the idea shimmered.

"*Good* morning, Mr. Fabb," I said with muted

cheerfulness, as I approached the circulation desk. "Good *morning*, Ms. Johansson," I then added, spotting her, the head librarian, standing in the office door in back.

"Good morning, *Gabe*," she said, coming out and heading for her place behind the desk. She was one of those great people who still acted like a friend of yours although, compared to hers, your brain was a bran muffin.

"Looking to improve your mind some more this weekend?" she inquired. "But is that possible? (she wonders). The Lévi-Strausses all are out, I fear, so could I recommend some early Gary Larsons? I think you'd find them *very* seminal, to say the least."

"I'm afraid the guy is too abstract for me, Ms. J." I said. "I need more pictures to explain the text. But thanks for the suggestion, anyway. In fact, I just came hoping for a word with Mr. Fabb."

I'd swung toward him as I said the last of that, and bore down on his name.

"Oh — morning, Gabe," he said, turning, looking up at me, at last. I thought he looked just dreadful. For one thing, he was thinner — or if not that, more drawn. His beard made it a little hard to tell, but still; his eyes seemed set back deeper in those hollows in his face.

He got up from his chair and shuffled the three closed books in front of him, as if they were three playing cards, and he was going to ask me to pick one of them. I recognized the Scribners paperback of *For Whom the Bell Tolls*, the exact same edition that I had in my room at home. I might have chosen it, but Mr. Fabb, he never made the offer. Nor did

166

he add those books to the ones on the wheeled cart at the end of the circulation desk.

"Do you have a minute, Mr. Fabb?" I said. He'd started to push the cart away from both the desk and me, as if he hadn't even heard what I'd just said to Ms. Johansson.

"What? Oh, yes. I guess," he said. "If you like, just come along while I take care of shelving these." He didn't sound enthusiastic. Or antagonistic, either. He seemed, as almost always, preoccupied and neutral.

Actually, I liked what he'd suggested fine. We'd be removed from where the action was. Maybe we'd communicate — like, man-to-boyfriend.

I decided I'd start off on pleasant common ground, that recent drug-test scene we'd both been party to. As he pushed his cart toward the stacks, I told him how relieved I'd been to see him, and the other men. How if they'd been two minutes later, they might have heard me babbling the Fourth Amendment while a half a dozen white-clad thugs were trying to wring a sample out of me above a sink, or something. That was jollying him along; I'm such a card.

"You would have been within your rights," he said, ignoring my attempt at levity, as usual, "in claiming the protection of Article IV. If there ever was a good example of an unreasonable search and seizure, it was what was taking place right there. Although I have my doubts that Dr. Leeds believes the Bill of Rights applies to kids at all."

"I know some *kids* who don't think they have any rights," I said.

"Of course," he said. "Their parents bring them

up to think that. They try to give them what they call 'responsibilities' — which usually are simply jobs they make them do. But when it comes to rights, *they're* all reserved for those who can afford them. And 'have paid their dues,' they say."

He straightened up and stared at me. His forehead shone, as if he'd started sweating.

" 'Unalienable rights,' our founding fathers called them. 'The pursuit of happiness,' " he said. "Have you ever thought about the meaning of those words, Gabe?"

"I don't know," I said. "Probably not really." Already, we had veered off course, gone in a direction other than the one I'd planned to follow.

"We spend our lives *pursuing* happiness," he said, now looking past my ear, above my shoulder, off into another distance. "Jumping over, skirting 'round the barriers — *impediments* — our fellow man, *society*, keeps putting in our way. Sometimes" — he nodded, solemnly — "in our frustration, on the borders of despair, we find it necessary to take further steps. In order to continue our pursuit of happiness we have to undertake the abolition of the forms and symbols of tyranny. It takes a few good men . . . How many signers of the Declaration were there? Fifty-some? How many dunkers at the Boston Tea Party? How many Patrick Henrys in the House of Burgesses?" He smiled; that caught me by surprise.

" '*Unalienable* rights,' " he said again, now back to standard-serious. "And that means rights not capable of being taken from your ownership, supposedly. By anyone, at any time. You have the *right* to pursue happiness, Gabe, not just a chance to, if you're lucky, if they let you, someday, maybe. Happiness!! Along with life and liberty, the three most precious gifts bestowed on man."

It was weird to hear him say that, in his usual not-happy tone of voice, and wearing his un-joyful face.

"When you're my age," I said, "you're still just kind of sorting through the possibilities. Trying to find out which varieties of happiness are real, and which are . . . well, *mirages.*"

"Just don't you go and swallow other people's definitions," he advised me. "That's half the trouble with the people in this town. They've put their faith in masks and monuments. Things that they can point with pride to, symbols of a fancied specialness. They think that *things* can make them happy."

He twisted up his face into a shape I'd never seen it in before. He had a sort of grotesque clownish look. Good Lord, I thought, he's going to tell a joke. He's going to jolly *me* along — be a card, himself.

"Why can't you kids be more like *downtown*, anyway?" he asked, with mock severity. "We've put a lot of money into both of you."

Before I could reply, he'd pushed his cart around a corner, down another aisle between two stacks of books. The cart ran quietly on rubber wheels, on padded indoor-outdoor carpeting. I sent a chuckle just ahead of me, as I went after him.

"That," I said, as I came up to where he'd stopped again, "reminds me of some stuff my mother said." What I planned to say might not exactly *fit* into the conversation, but with him you had to force a little, sometimes. I wanted him to feel that in a lot of ways my mother was an ally, on his side. That'd make it easier for him to go to her, I thought. If only he could feel less isolated, better understood. . . .

"She agrees you can't just *make* kids do the so-called 'right' thing all the time," I said. "Construct their attitudes and personalities as if they were a bunch of buildings, like you said. For instance, she believes they aren't going to 'just say no' because it's safe or smart or good advice. Especially when their own parents aren't saying no to dirty deals and finding loopholes in the laws, and cheating on insurance claims. Or to lying (called, 'mis-speaking' or 'mis-stating'), or to kickbacks, or to favoritism. Or to lots of different kinds of . . . well, *excesses*." That sounded slightly forced and formal, but I hadn't wanted to get too specific with a guy who could be doubly addicted.

"But she also thinks some parents may be getting conscious of connections," I went on. "Seeing that the stuff their kids do has its causes in the adult world. Seeing that their kids are *people*, not just smaller windup toys that they can program different ways."

"Your mother thinks that's happening?" His tone said *surely-you-are-kidding-me.* He turned to me, now bent way over, a book in either hand. "In *Dustin?*"

"Yes," I said. "Just barely starting to. She thought that all those parents going to the school to stop the drug test was significant. It wasn't just herself, and you, and Mr. Koch. The thing is, Mr. Fabb" — I tried to sound *exceptionally* mature, right up there on his level — "my mother gets to see a lot of people, doing what she does. Here, it's like, more *specialized*. I don't mean the library's an ivory tower or anything, but it *is* a little different than the streets. You ought to go and more or less swap points of view with her, sometime."

"Yes, probably I *should* do that," he said. I barely could believe my ears; this hadn't been so hard at all. He really was somewhat susceptible to reason, and to good advice.

"You're right." He went right on. "I don't see many different kinds of people, or hear those different points of view. My tendency is not to socialize a lot. I like to do a job and make my own decisions, independently. Based on my perceptions and beliefs." He ducked his head and turned away. "Like Michael Jordan."

That's what I thought I heard him mumble, anyway. It really set me back. Llewellyn Fabb an NBA fan? Thinking he was like Air Jordan, different ways? Was he going to slam dunk *Catcher in the Rye*? Get in Norman Mailer's face? Hello, Hallucination City. We are coming in for a landing — or, more likely, one terrific crash.

I should have headed out of there right then, left well enough alone. In part, my problem was I couldn't find some little thing to say before "goodbye," an exit line.

So, instead, I stood and babbled. To fill the silence — and also, probably, to try to make myself look good. I told him all about The What-not in the Parking Lot: the night Lafountain and myself took on the Mother Mob.

But my story didn't seem to either please him or

amuse him. What it did was send him right back to the soapbox.

"Typical," he said. "Those people think that anything they do is made all right by what they feel is their own pious and/or patriotic motivation. Any time they don't like what is written in the Constitution or the laws that Congress passes, they just claim that they're obeying '*higher* laws.' They act as if they know exactly what God's thinking is on every issue — and Thomas Jefferson's as well. So anything they do is justified, if not entirely legal, according to the books. Certainly, they're never *wrong*." He shook his head. "Those people." The sound he made was unexpected, and most impolite.

"But still," I countered weakly. I was now devoid of fresh material. "There *were* the ones who came and stopped the drug test. *They* stood up for the law, I'd say."

"Huh," he said. He picked up two more books and stared down at their spines. He looked as if he *hated* those two titles. "I bet you half of them were there because they thought their own kid might test positive. What would the neighbors think of *that*? Bunch of goddam hypocrites is what they are!"

"Yes — well," I said. Everything that Dori'd told me now seemed right. *Losing it*, it seemed to me, described his situation pretty well. It wasn't that the guy was totally off base, that everything he said was nutsy. It was more a matter of degree, and emphasis. Of "raving," as she'd said.

"I really hope you *do* talk to my mother." I decided that I'd try to close with that. "She'd be *really* interested, I know, in everything you have to say."

And how. Desperately, I added something that I'd said before, but inside-out this time. "Maybe her perspectives need an overhaul. She'd be the first one to admit" — I forced a little laugh — "that everybody kids themselves at times, just sees the things they want to see." I waved a hand and shrugged. "You know?"

Llewellyn Fabb had started to hit the spine of the book in his left hand with the spine of the book in his right, as if he had some thing between the two of them he wanted flattened, crushed, destroyed.

I waved again. "Well, see you later," I concluded. And I left him by himself, to do whatever he was doing.

25
D. RANKIN ORRIFICE

On the Thursday after that, I found myself escorting Dori down the first floor hall of Dustin High. Our destination was the auditorium; it was not a voluntary trip. Like all the other junior values/social studies classes, ours was to attend a lecture by our congressman. His name: D. Rankin Orrifice; his subject: Love of Country.

I used the word "escorting" very much on purpose; I had my hand on Dori's arm, just above the elbow. This was permitted by the Hall Rules promulgated by the principal that fall. Holding hands was *not* permitted; arms-around-each-other was a felony, of course. You were allowed, however, both to touch and also punch a person in between the elbow and the shoulder, in the halls. And so it sometimes seemed, on breaks between the classes, as if the school was full of youthful-looking undercover cops, with female prisoners in tow. "Come with me" and "Right this way, please" were the things you found you felt like saying, as the guy in one of those strange twosomes.

Sometimes, keeping up her end in this weird play-let, Dori'd duck her head and try to hide her face behind an open notebook, or in *Dust Devils*. But on this Thursday she was walking normally and giving me the latest on her dad's activities.

" . . . going on these errands after dinner," she was saying. "Picking up some part or other for the car. Or he says he's thinking of taking up oil painting and he needs to check out different art supply stores. Of course he means the big ones in the city, so naturally he's gone for hours. I just go to bed."

"Well, what's he doing really, do you think?" I asked her. I didn't want to say what *I* thought.

"Who knows?" she said. She shrugged, making like she didn't even care. "If he's getting bombed, he's learned to do it quietly. The getting-in-the-house part, anyway. I never hear him coming in. One thing, though — he's much more up and down, like, Mr. Mood Swings. I can't believe I used to whine about his never showing his emotions."

"I'm pretty sure he hasn't turned up at the clinic, yet," I said.

"You think your mother would have told you, necessarily?" she asked.

I thought that over. "No," I said. "I guess she wouldn't have."

And Dori nodded. Dori knew my mom.

Varney Poole was standing by the door we planned to enter.

"You're not going to take attendance, are you, Mr. Poole?" asked Dori, as a matter of principle. Varney had already told us, twice, we had to sit together as a class, so he could do exactly that.

"I really should go home and do my nails, this period," she added quickly, fluttering a hand between them. "As you can plainly see, I chipped the — "

"Fourth or fifth row center," Varney butted in to say. "I'm sure the congressman won't mind, Dorinda."

"Ooh," she said. "You mean he's, like, a *liberal*? I thought he might be when I heard the title of his talk. It's 'Love-in in the Country,' isn't it?"

She gave her dumb-blonde giggle and batted her long lashes at him madly, but Varney only shook his head and, coplike, waved us into the auditorium. He winked at me as we went by.

The place was pretty full, already. What had happened was that certain members of the senior and the sophomore classes had petitioned Mr. Morehead. They'd said that "Love of Country" was a value *all* the kids should take an interest in. And besides, some seniors said, they'd have the right to vote in the next election, and Orrifice, their present congressman, would certainly be up for re-election. They wanted to "begin to formulate informed opinions on the guy." Or so my source of senior information, Donald Cremin, swore to me they'd said.

Given all that pressure, Morehead ruled that any

176

student was *permitted* (though only juniors were *required*) to attend the speech. You can guess how that went over with a lot of teachers. Somehow they *knew* there's nothing that produces patriotic fervor in a kid much faster than the chance to miss an hour test on *Silas Marner*, say.

And they were right. The atmosphere inside the auditorium was downright festive. There were a lot of kids in there who felt they'd put one over on the system. I guessed it hadn't hit them yet that now they'd have to listen to a *speech*. And that the speaker wasn't Rodney Dangerfield or Richard Pryor.

I looked around as we went down the aisle. There were even lots of teachers there, and people in the balcony, like Donald Cremin, almost in spite of himself. Donald told me later that his English teacher, Ralph R. Runcible, had just dismissed his decimated class.

"If Mr. Morehead feels you people needn't go to English class," he told the ones who showed, "then *he* can be the one to tell your parents why your verbals look like bowling scores. I'd say that *somebody's* priorities are showing."

And then he'd sniffed, so Donald said.

Up on the stage, and facing us, were Mrs. Teagle, Dr. Leeds and Mr. Nevins, two empty chairs and, naturally, the flag. Leeds and Nevins were both smiling, chatting back and forth, each with one leg flung informally across the other knee. The message they were sending was: Hey — isn't this great fun?

Mrs. Teagle looked a whole lot less amused. Perhaps, I thought, she'd got a glimpse of BeBe Rector's

177

bright cerise, but partly lace and somewhat see-through, bra. BeBe'd planned, we knew, to open up her shirt and flash it and its contents at the speaker, partway through his talk. But she hadn't counted on the school directors being on the platform, with probably the principal to come. So Dori's whispered guess, to me, was that she'd chicken out — though maybe still give private, surreptitious, giggled-over peeks to girls on either side of her. Which *I* thought maybe Mrs. T. had gotten in on. She had an old school get-thee-to-the-woodshed look about her.

For all his casual demeanor, it's fair to say that Leeds's stock in town had taken quite a tumble since the day that drug-test deal unraveled. Of course some parents gave him credit for a darn good try ("Look! You want to help those kids, or not?"). But many others thought he'd gone too far. Even the ratlike *Dustin Times* dove overboard: "That wasn't *our* idea," their piefaced editors exclaimed.

I wondered at the time if Leeds connected me to what had happened. He must have known the parents had been called by someone. All those dads and moms could not have simply *felt*, at once, that they were *needed* in the boys' and girls' rooms down at school. But would he ever in the world suspect yrs. truly? Maybe not, I thought. An A to F would be a far, far better possibility. Podesta, G., who after all was there, about to take the test when Mr. Jerry Koch and them came in, could hardly be a suspect. It was even possible, I tried to tell myself, that Leeds did not remember that we'd . . . quarreled. Or that he'd promised me at least one truckload's worth of trouble. What kind of adult school director, after all, would stoop to taking, like, revenge on some mere school child?

A door behind the platform finally opened, and through it stepped a man of middle size, but less than middle age. And he didn't just come in, he made an Entrance. Our principal came two steps after, the way Prince Philip always does.

Leeds and Nevins bounded to their feet, all sugar-faced and smiley; their hands, chest-high, became a blur of world-class clapping. Mrs. Teagle didn't match their smoke. She rose a lot more slowly, and in two installments: tilt and push. Perhaps she also grunted. And her old school style of clapping was so ladylike, it almost seemed . . . reluctant. Could the woman be a Democrat, I wondered? But anyway, there was The Man, his Entrance made, before us.

D. Rankin Orrifice was certainly well-rounded. I'd know the half of it before I'd ever seen him: He'd been a ReallyFineSmallCollege man, a choral singer, decent doubles player, crack debater, horseman, lawyer and investment banker. And now I had the opportunity to know he *looked* well-rounded, too.

If not exactly fat, the congressman *did* fill his skin to near capacity. And over it he wore a suit of smooth, well-tailored gabardine, three pieces worth: the coat, and pants, and vest, the color of a coffee with two creams. The overall impression that he gave was one of gently curving slopes. It crossed my mind that if you put him in a lard fight, every blob that hit him would slide slowly off, and end up on the rug. Don't ask me why I thought that, I just did.

I also thought he looked a tad self-satisfied. The expression on his closely-shaven, big-chinned face suggested that he didn't merely *get* the joke, but that, perhaps, he'd written it. And even worse, his hair was full and dry and natural, but perfectly in place — the way mine never was. In other words, the guy had *power* hair, and I was jealous of it. Small of me, I know, but there you have it.

While I was noticing all this, I joined my fellow students, and the teachers, in some clapping of our own. A few extremists had jumped up to do this, just as Leeds and Nevins had, but most of us stayed seated out of laziness — or arrogance, indifference, or hostility. None of these were underrepresented in our school community, the faculty included. So, pretty soon, the standers-up sat down, and Mr. Morehead went behind the lecturn.

Basically, he played it safe, not overdoing praise, but ending " . . . now, to talk on 'Love of Country,' I am honored to present a man who loves and serves his country well, Representative D. Rankin Orrifice, our congressman."

Leeds and Nevins tried to lead us in some further, frantic patty-caking, and D.R.O. stepped forward. He slid a deck of index cards from one suit pocket, smooth as if his name were Mississippi Slim.

"My fellow young Americans . . . " is how he started. He had an "educated" speaking voice, the kind you overhear explaining sailboat racing, or telling someone dressed in bright green pants just where the perfect "unspoiled" place to go is, nowadays.

The early sections of his talk were perfectly okay. Hell, why shouldn't I admit it? — they were *good*. Just to give you an idea: He pointed out how weirdly wonderful it was that all those different major talents, such as Adams (S. & J.), Tom Paine, Ben Franklin, Thomas Jefferson and Hamilton, and Washington and Madison and Dr. Rush, and a couple of Lees and Morrises et cetera were *all* around when they were needed most to (1) conceptualize and (2&3) both fight for and then put to work our principles and early government.

He then went on, still going strong, to underline the difference between the freedoms that we have and the tyrannies of different sorts that threaten and assail them, still. He said (and, boy, did I agree!) that democratic principles are nobler by far than any other governmental principles, that they depend on both equality and liberty for all, and thus must not be simply cherished and remarked upon but also deeply understood, and worked for — and examined, also spread. He argued we must never make excuses for, and so condone, the tyrannies of left and right we see in other countries. He also said the social contract that we have with one another, and with all humanity, is not without its costs — and we should try to meet them cheerfully, and bravely and humanely.

Maybe other people's eyes glazed over while he said all that, but not Podesta, G.'s. *I* was laying heavy stares on Mrs. Teagle, Leeds and Nevins. Stares that positively *dripped* with meaning. "Are you listening?" my eyeballs said.

181

But then, while I was still in midstare, so to speak, the speech just came apart.

Here is how it seemed to me: The speaker hadn't listened to *himself*. Fast as you could say "The U.S. Constitution," he was busily explaining that it was okay to lie and break the law, assume all sorts of powers for yourself, and tell the people one thing, do another, *provided* that you really loved the country and detested communism. Love of country, this guy seemed to say, was like a super-value, that could override all others.

"*Doink*," my jaw went. And another "value" bit the dust, snuck-up-behind and mugged by its interpreter.

Concluding, Orrifice expressed his great delight at being in our school and town, beneath the famous Dustin dome. He said it was a truly visionary thing, that dome, and it provided living proof that our technology and will could make the world a better and a safer place for all Americans.

When he was finished, everybody clapped — some hard and long, some soft and short. Orrifice had done the job in under thirty minutes, so a lot of grateful kids were surely working on ideas for how to spend the half an hour that had dropped into their day as if from heaven. That group clapped hard, but also short, I would imagine.

But . . . wait. The speaker hadn't moved. Oh, gross; oh, groan. And then he said that he'd be glad to answer any *questions* that we had. Oh, please, *don't anybody ask one*, lots of people prayed.

And for a little time thereafter no hands rose. The speaker looked from left to right. He muttered some-

182

thing and the front row giggled nervously. At last a *teacher* raised his hand.

"Blah-blah, blah-blah-blah with Star Wars?" he inquired.

The answer, which concerned "the President's Strategic Defense Initiative," took a great deal longer, just as you'd expect.

So, then a brownie senior asked: "Blah-blah-blah-blah in 1988?"

Another careful answer came. Summed-up, it was: "Don't ever count me out, kid."

Now, a half a dozen hands were up. *Sheesh.* Another boring question brought an even duller answer. What the hell, I thought. We were going to sit there anyway. Maybe it was time for some democracy in action, some freedom of expression, like. I stuck my arm up high.

Dori whispered viciously, "You *idiot!*"

The congressman was pointing to our neighborhood. *Me?* I pointed at my chest and raised my brows. He nodded.

"Sir," I said, "blah-blah-blah condone blah-blah-blah-blah-blah private government blah-blah-blah our foreign policy?"

His answer, delivered in a phony-patient pedagogic tone of voice, added up to (simply) this: The ends *had* justified the means; a bunch of wrongs *can* make a right.

Stunner. Suppose (I thought) the mothers of the world got hold of that one?

Very shortly afterwards, the questions ended. Mr. Orrifice just waved at us and walked away, not even waiting for applause; Dr. Leeds went, too, and got the door for him. And Mr. Morehead *strolled* back to the microphone. Dr. Leeds re-entered and resumed his seat. What the hell was going on? we wondered.

Well, we soon found out.

Apparently, so Morehead said, the "program" wasn't over. There was another — one more — part to come. What we would shortly see — be shown — was how this sort of program would be done behind the Iron Curtain. Mr. Orrifice had written and rehearsed what Morehead called a "simulation." He would soon return — but in the role of commissar instead of congressman. And with him he would have — Mr. Morehead's voice got deep and ominous — "the sort of escort commissars require." We shouldn't be alarmed, but should pay close attention, Morehead said.

Almost at once, the door behind the stage flew open and through it came (or, rather, *strutted*) . . . could it be? Yes — Mr. Orrifice! But altered, overhauled, *transformed*. Instead of perfect, tailored, gabardine and wing-tipped Florsheim shoes, he wore a gross, gray, double-breasted suit, too tight around the waist and just plain bad across the shoulders, and black, clod-hopping oxfords on his feet. His hair had been moussed down and combed across the top from left to right; the collar of his shirt appeared to be too tight, one tab of it curled upwards. He looked as if he'd never even *heard* a joke he liked.

26
AUDIENCE
PARTICIPATION GAMES

Perhaps it was the shock; I'm not quite sure. But people started laughing. He just looked so *ridiculous*. Someone else might not have, but he did.

Pretty quickly, though, the laughter all died down. D. Rankin hadn't cracked a smile — and we began to pay attention to what else was happening. Down both side aisles had marched a line of soldiers, carrying rifles. Their caps and uniforms were not American. They really did look foreign, and none of them was smiling. They all had red stars on their caps. They stood with feet apart, facing toward the audience, spaced out along the length of both side aisles.

Orrifice began his second rap. He did it really well, I'll give him that. He must have acted some, in college. He didn't try to use an accent, but his cadence was much different than before, and the way his sentences were formed. He spoke about the "motherland" and what our duty to it was. He trashed imperialists and capitalists and blamed them for starvation and disease around the world. "Liberation" was a major theme.

When he stopped speaking, none of us knew what to do. *Applause* seemed inappropriate to us Americans, but still, he'd done a real good acting job, and so you didn't want to hiss and boo — even if you dared to. And, too, you felt that what he'd done had been authentic, that that's the way it is in a one-party state. So, like all the other people in that room, I sat there doing nothing.

Turned out that that was fine. The program wasn't over. Our "commissar" proclaimed there'd now be questions. We should feel "entirely free" to ask him anything we wanted to.

"Beginning now," he ordered. And then he pointed right at me and said, "First you, young man. I'm sure you have an interesting question. Anything you want."

Of course I *didn't* have a question ready. I began to shake my head. But then I thought: Come on, cooperate. Be the good sport that your parents brought you up to be. And so I did as he had told me to, and pretended that I *was* "entirely free" to ask him anything.

"How can you defend blah-blah, the use of blah-blah-blah-blah-blah Afghanistan, blah-blah-blah also blah-blah-blah Sakharov?"

Well. No sooner had that question left my lips than Orrifice barked orders left and right. I didn't

186

get exactly what he said; Lafountain thought it wasn't even English. But anyway, the first two soldiers on each side snapped to it. They gave their rifles to their nearest comrades and then jogged around to the front of the room and started up the inner aisles.

Qué pasa, anyway? thought Craig Podesta's marginally bilingual son.

They got to the fourth row and entered it, pushing their way in, like late arrivals at the movies. But there weren't any empty seats to head for. The row was filled with people from our values class; those dudes were coming after *me*.

I kept my optimistic cool. "This must be something that they planned," I muttered to Dorinda. "They're only *actors*, after all."

And as the first guy reached me, coming from my left, I decided that I'd play along authentically, be like a grade-A dissident.

"Don't touch me, lousy Commie so-and-so's. . . ." I started with a pseudo-snarl. Some classmates giggled at the words I used instead of "so-and-so's." I felt the soldiers, fellow actors, would respect my methods.

But before I knew what hit me, I'd been spun around, bent over, grabbed in such a way that both my wrists were seized and both my arms were twisted up behind my back. In that position, I was pushed on down the row and out into the aisle. It really felt as if one arm, at least, was getting dislocated at the shoulder.

"Jesus! Hey, my arm. . . !"

I wasn't acting then, nor was I making an attempt

to keep it down. Some dumb son-of-a-bitch, some small-time Kevin Costner, had simulated much too well. I wanted him to stop; I may have called him names as I requested that. But he hadn't gone the full route yet, I soon found out.

Once we'd reached the aisle, he gave his buddy my left arm to hold. Which gave *him* one free hand, or fist, to slam into my neck and then into my stomach.

Of course I quickly shrugged those punches off and started with my Indiana Jones/Mike Tyson imitation . . . yeah, yeah, bullshit. The truth is that the first punch took me to another world of hurt. My knees gave way; I swear I saw a flash behind my eyes. And then the second punch, by knocking out my wind as well, stole every bit of strength and courage that I had and put them somewhere else, a place I didn't even care about.

The only two thoughts in my head were: Breathe, somehow; and Am I going to die?

Now, completely doubled over, I was held up by my two-man military escort, the other two behind them. Semiconscious, staggering, I had no sense of all the turbulence around me, nor am I sure I even *heard* the shouting and the grunting and the screams that (so they tell me) shortly followed. The next thing that I *really* knew was when, flat on my back on the floor of the seventh row, I opened up my eyes and looked at Dori's worried face, above me. She'd straddled me, was lifting up my rib cage rhythmically, helping me to breathe. And I *was* breathing. It appeared I wasn't going to die.

I'd become aware of sounds by then. I think I

knew there was a riot going on. But I didn't know until days later, really, how the thing had come to be, and grown, and finally ended. What I can tell you now is pieced together from the stories that I got from lots of different witnesses: Lafountain on the main floor, Donald Cremin in the balcony, Varney Poole, participant, and others.

I guess when I was pushed into the aisle and punched like that, almost everyone assumed it was an act — one part of a rehearsed routine. Ronnie Gervais may have wished that it was real, and other people probably thought well of G. Podesta simulating agony. Lafountain swore he *knew* the soldier'd pulled his punches ("It looked so fake-o, Gabe; I swear"), and that I wasn't hurt at all. In fact, as far as I can tell, the only person in the place, other than Dorinda, to make the smallest move on my behalf was Varney Poole.

No sooner was that first punch thrown than Varney left his seat and started chugging down the aisle. He couldn't get there fast enough to keep the second one from landing, but a moment after it he'd grabbed that soldier by the arm and had started giving him the word on who to get his goddamn hands off. Varney had correctly guessed that all those guys *were* soldiers — guardsmen, actually, not regular army guys — recruited for this "play" from our state guard by Orrifice. Varney knew that actors, other than S. Penn, perhaps, don't punch that good.

The soldiers didn't go for Varney's attitude at all. Lafountain said he thought that Varney should have used his symptoms-causes speech on them, instead.

That way, he said, they might have nodded off and simply dropped me. But this other, more aggressive line did nothing but provoke them. Soldier two grabbed hold of Varney, so's to make him take *his* hands off soldier one. And, I guess, at that point Varney went berserk.

Lafountain said the scene reminded him of this one time he'd tried to make some frosting in his mother's kitchen. He'd taken the electric beater, a device that he was not familiar with, and cranked it up to high and stuck it in the bowl of frosting stuff. One moment everything in Cookie World was neat and orderly, the way his mother liked it, but in the next one total hell broke loose. Frosting mix began to fly around the kitchen. Lafountain yanked the beater back and tried to grab the bowl, but fumbled it, causing further food to fly. His mother, hearing muffled curses over kitchen horror-sounds of falling objects, possibly appliances gone wild, came running. So did their two dogs, both German shepherds. The last three entries all were yelping, said Lafountain; there was also jumping up and down.

Varney was the beater in this present scene, I guess, and soldier two became the frosting mix. We'd known our Mr. Poole's idea of fun was climbing sheer rock walls, but none of us had ever stopped to think how strong you have to be to do that and enjoy it. Or how courageous and in shape, as well. What Varney did there in the auditorium was climb up one side of old two and down the other one, leaving him as flat as what, on Sundays in our house, we pour the syrup on.

190

When soldiers one and three and four observed this unexpected (I suppose) event, they moved to help their buddy. And *that* inspired other teachers, and some students, too, to feel that in the absence of a UN force, there was a role that they could fill, as peacekeepers.

Some of these, of course, turned out to be the sort of people who believe that peace is kept most easily when there's a winning war to base it on. Before he climbed down off his seat and shoved his way to Dori's side to help her drag me into shelter in row seven, Lafountain saw the bull-like form of Ratsy Rizzo make a roaring charge straight down the aisle and, staying low and using the techniques peculiar to the nose guards of this world, begin to straighten up and scatter military bodies, left and right.

Donald Cremin, Mr. Bird's Eye in the balcony, said that Ratsy's charge set off stage two (or three, or four) in what was soon to be a full-fledged riot. The soldiers in the two side aisles, seeing colleagues bouncing here and there like tenpins, decided they should get involved themselves. Logically enough, they tried to just shove down the rows in front of them. Bad mistake, as it turned out. Those rows, you see, were full of people, standing, trying to get a better view, lots of whom were high school girls who, as everybody knows, are taught to scream when someone touches them (*kidding, Dori, kidding*).

Their screams, in any case, did more than just contribute to the atmosphere. As you may also know: If you're a high school guy, and a girl you date, or think you'd like to date, starts screaming, and she knows you're in the room, you've only got one choice. You saddle up and get to just exactly where she is, *muy pronto*.

So, that means lots of guys were shortly shouting "Hi-o, Silver!" (or some acceptable equivalent, like: "What the fuck! Hey, Wendy!"), and then proceeding to push frantically in one direction or another, meeting soldiers on the way, and sometimes punching them.

But while all *this* was going on (said Donald) there was also lots of action on the stage. D. Rankin Orrifice had stayed right where he was, at first, behind the microphone. His mouth gaped open, as in disbelief, while he observed his program turn to pandemonium. But he didn't say a single word to stop it, either in his role as commissar, or as what he really was, our congressman.

This was apparently too much for R.D. Morehead, Principal. When shoulder-tapping and suggesting seemed to get him nowhere, he simply picked D. Rankin up, quite bodily, and cast him to one side. This made it possible for him to grab the microphone and try to get the crowd's attention.

"Boys and girls!" he cried. "You . . . *men!* Membahs of the *faculty*. . . !"

No one paid the slightest heed, said Donald, but Mr. Orrifice, recovering his balance, then decided (Donald guessed) that congressmen did not put up with being tossed aside, like trash, by principals. And so he stretched his arms out, bent, and motored back across the stage. And when he reached the podium, he gave R.D. a vicious, double-handed shove that sent him flying into Dr. Leeds.

192

That might not have been *too* bad, except that Leeds had seized the flag — perhaps to use it as a weapon, if he had to (Donald thought), or possibly to merely wave it, for attention. So when old Morehead rocketed across the stage and into him, the force of the collision spun him half around, and naturally Old Glory with him.

It — or, I should say, the pole that it was on *and* it — thus came to whack our Mrs. Teagle squarely on the broadest part of her, and send her flying into Mr. Nevins. A moment later he was sprawled flat on his back, with Mrs. T. on top of him, and squirming.

By that time, Mr. Doremus, an assistant custodian at the school who is also the secretary of the local Legion Post, had made his contribution to the scene. Hearing sounds of rioting from where he was, down in the basement, he came up the back stairs into the area behind the stage, found the cassette with the national anthem on it, and stuck that in the PA system. Of course it then took him a while to hit the proper switches to turn *off* the on-stage mike and get the other amplifier going. So what he ended up actually *playing* was the last six bars of "The Star-Spangled Banner," and then the rest of the music on that particular tape. Donald said he thought those songs — "Stars and Stripes Forever," "The Thunderer," and "The Notre Dame Victory March" — might have added some pizzaz to all the brawling.

"Even I," he said, "a guy with hardly any fighting spirit whatsoever, always get a little rush of energy from martial music."

What finally caused hostilities to wind down and

then, at last, to end, is anybody's guess. Exhaustion was a factor, certainly. Also, I am pretty sure, some people must have started thinking "What the hell, exactly, is this all about?" But most of all, I think, it was the siren: Mrs. Teagle's "Scum-B-Gone."

After she had taken Betsy Ross's work across her ass, and flattened T. Hank Nevins under her, Mrs. Teagle scrambled to all-fours and grabbed her handbag from the floor. And from it she pulled out her key ring, which had a "Scum-B-Gone" attached to it. The thing had been a present from her daughter, who'd found it in the Home and Personal Security section of a big department store in the city where she lived and had bought one for herself and another for her mother. They work — as that one did that morning — on compressed air. Flick the safety off and press the button and at once these great *A-HOOGA!* howls begin, and then go on and on. They're meant to have a ten-block range; I promise you they filled that auditorium and much much more. Thieves and rapists fled the building, I presume; rioters stopped rioting and covered up their ears. By the time the last *A-HOOGA!* sounded, almost all the punchers and punchees had stopped competing, Donald said, and were standing there and panting, looking at each other.

And in the almost-silence after that, everybody heard the educated voice of Orrifice for one last time, concluding his remarks to Morehead, in a shriek: ". . . you damned, egregious, preternatural, gherkin-jerker, you!"

27
AFTER WORDS

My father kept me home from school, next day.
I'd gotten up and dressed at the regular time and
come down to the kitchen with the expectation that
I'd soon be out there bobbing on the vast and semi-
charted seas of knowledge, as per usual. Dori and
Lafountain had been over, night before, and Donald
Cremin had checked in by phone so, thanks to them,
I had a pretty good idea of all that had transpired
while I rested, horizontal, in the seventh row. But
still, I wanted to return and get back on the horse
that threw me, so to speak. It would be G. Podesta,
victim, drawn back to Dustin High School, historically the scene of many, many crimes.

I was a little stiff and sore — especially my
neck — but it wasn't really bad. I found I still could
shake my head and say with what I'd call a boyish-

brave-but-rueful smile, "To tell you guys the truth, I never saw the punches, either one — but I sure *felt* them." And then go on to grimace, slightly, touching the ugly-looking bruises that were right there, plain to see (provided that I wore a shirt without a collar, like my present blue and white one) and, tight-lipped, just accept the sympathy of one and all: juniors, seniors, sophomores, even teachers — blondes, brunettes and redheads. I'd tried all this before the bathroom mirror and, I swear to you, it *worked*.

But my father was determined that I wouldn't go. The man was plain dug-in. Unshakable. Impossible.

"No, no, no, no, no. Listen, bozo. This is one time I don't *want* for you to be a real good sport about it. Will you please just shut your mouth and go along with me on this? I think some other people ought to come to you, to *us*, to *me*. And your mother, the psychologist, agrees."

All the time my father was saying that, he was putting golf balls on the kitchen carpet, over ancient gravy stains and past a newly-fallen corn flake. Every day of his life he putts over a thousand balls, no matter where he is. He uses different styles and different *things* when he is practicing. He can putt better between his legs with an empty one liter Schweppes tonic-water bottle than the pro at your club can putt with a putter. He can probably putt better with an umbrella or a standing lamp, or certainly with what he was using right then, a tennis racquet. I've seen him make five ten-footers in a row with a *guitar*, for heaven's sake.

196

"What we're hoping, Gabe," my mother said, "is that maybe now a lot of people will start coming to their senses. About this whole values program. I don't know how serious the other injuries were, but — "

"Just that something like that could happen in the school at all," my father interrupted in the outraged tone he'd apparently adopted for the day. "In broad daylight. I'll be curious to see if anyone admits responsibility for this . . . this *program*. I'm sure that once-and-future fink, that Orrifice, will say they've never had this kind of trouble anywhere before, and he couldn't have *imagined* that any of those men would go so far as to *assault* a student. No matter *what* the provocation."

And he snorted, which produced a mini-miracle: He missed a putt. Which made him snort again.

"And speaking of . . . well, provocation," my mother said to me. "That was something that we meant to ask you, yesterday. Granted that no matter what you said, the soldier had no right to hit you . . . that's still a question that is bound to be brought up — "

" — possibly in court . . ." my father stuck in there.

"What *did* you say to him, exactly?" she inquired.

"Gee," I said, "in *court*? You aren't serious. I don't want to go to any court." I paused; I thought; I possibly remembered. "I don't think I know, exactly. What I said, I mean. I was only kidding, anyway. You gotta remember I thought the guy was an actor, and it was all some big joke — their coming after me, I mean. If I'd known he was an actual

197

soldier — or a member of the state militia, or the National Gaurd, or whatever he was — I probably wouldn't have said anything at all." I snapped my fingers. "Look. I want to call Dori anyway, and tell her I'm not going to school. Maybe she'll remember what I said, okay?"

They both agreed to that, so I trotted into the den, for privacy, and got Dorinda on the phone. She said that she'd come over, after school. And just as I had feared, she did remember.

When I rejoined the kitchen group, my mother, quite predictably, said, "Well. . . ?"

I made a face. "It was . . . a little out of taste. I'm pretty sure you guys don't want to hear it. You see, in *context* it was different — like in plays they say all sorts of words, and it isn't as if anybody *means* exactly what — "

"Come on," my father said. He covered up my mother's ears. "Just *say* it."

I muttered, "LousyCommiemotherfuckers," really fast.

"What?" my father shrieked. He staggered two steps back. I blushed. "Your son," he told my mother, "suggested that the man was Marxist-Oedipal."

"How grossly unimaginative," my mother said, pretending to stifle a yawn. "You'd never hear that on a golf course, would you?"

"Never," said my father. "Oedipal's a *baseball* word. Say it, and the umpire throws you out of the game, though. But if they say it in therapy, you schedule an extra hour, right? But, anyway. . . ."

The phone rang; just as well, in my opinion. My

parents aren't hung up on the "bad language" issue, and when I was younger I might have taken small advantage of that fact. But not at this stage of my life. Colorful speech has its place, and "the words" can qualify as colorful, at times. But overuse can fade the color out of anything — clothes *or* language, equally — as well as cause it to become real boring. Frankly, I like *being able* to say whatever I want to, but not *having to*.

From my mother's half of the phone conversation, I deduced that the caller was another mother — Debi Regan's, she was in my class. And that Deb had suffered "bruises" in the melee. It seemed she'd been knocked over the backs of the seats in the row in front of her, and had landed on a shoulder and her sassafras. My mother agreed that the whole incident has been "perfectly disgusting" and said that I, too, was "being kept out of" the school "for the time being."

Of course as soon as she hung up, I complained about being made to sound like a six-year-old, but I'd barely gotten the complaint out of my mouth and started to ask her what on earth she'd meant by "for the time being," when there came a banging on the old back door. My father put his racquet on the table and wandered down the little hall to answer it. When he returned, he was, to my surprise, accompanied by one Llewellyn Fabb. And it appeared his mood had swung to "agitated," Llewellyn Fabb's, that is.

In spite of that, he nodded to my mother, said, "Good morning, Pattie," before he turned and put the urgency on me.

"Gabe," he said. "Dori told me you were staying out of school. Are you *all right*? You're *sure*?"

Of course I told him I was fine, terrific, wonderful. I even stood and did a little dance to prove it — and to try to lighten up the atmosphere a speck. He didn't laugh and start in with the country-rhythmic clappin' and a-stompin' bit, but at least he did relax enough to take a chair and say "Yes, thanks" to "Coffee, Llew?" from Mom.

When he got his mug, he looked at both my parents, back and forth. First one and then the other. They knew each other from the library and because, with me and Dori fairly long-term daters, there'd been a lot of back-and-forths concerning staying-over and, especially before I drove, who was going to pick "them" up. But the three of them were not, like, social friends; no one was with Mr. Fabb, I didn't think. And now he looked to me as if he might be making up his mind about my parents, deciding whether they were both mature and bright enough to handle what he had to say.

"You know they set Gabe up?" he finally said to them. "You realize that yesterday's . . ." He drew his lips back from his teeth. ". . . *imbroglio* was planned, somehow?"

My father countered with that easygoing smile of his.

"You reckon so?" he said. Hanging out with golfers makes him talk like that, sometimes. But chances are he learned "imbroglio" at Duke.

"I'm sure of it," said Mr. Fabb. He spoke authoritatively and briskly now. His empty hand was doing finger exercises on the tabletop.

200

"I haven't any proof, of course," he said, "but I don't need it. I know the people in the picture — or *about* them, anyway — and how they think and operate. They wanted Gabe and all the other kids to get the message, loud and clear."

"Namely, that he should . . . shut up?" my mother asked. "About the sorts of things — "

"That he should — yes — shut up," said Mr. Fabb. I don't think he even noticed he had interrupted her. "And much, much more. That he should not write letters, interfere with vigilantes, associate with users, criticize and act against school policies (even if illegal), or even know about, and possibly make use of, birth control devices." And he laughed, I think, a single "Hah!"

"And even *more*," he said. He jumped to his feet and came and stood behind me. I hoped he didn't think that I'd been using "birth control devices" on or with his daughter, Dori.

"This Gabe," he said, "he seems to think he's free to practice all the liberties our laws allow him to, and use all their protections, too. Well, they can't stand it. He is" — he put a hand down on my shoulder, which was the first time he had ever touched me, I believe — "he is, as far as they're concerned, a troublemaker, and so he and all the other kids were sent a message, yesterday, that troublemakers *will* get hurt." He walked back to his chair and sat, again.

My parents passed a look between them I could not interpret. It could have meant "What did I tell you?", but it also could have meant "Come *on*."

"I'd kind of thought the situation was improving," said my father. "That even nationwide the atmosphere had gotten . . . brighter, you could say. Seems like folks are seeing that it's bad to mess around with people's basic rights. Their right to say or read the things they choose to, to manage their own bodies, stuff like that."

"Well, yes and no to that," said Mr. Fabb. He glanced at my mother. "But what you have to realize in this case is: Power has peculiar properties. A normal person can accept the ebb and flow of it — win a few, lose a few, that kind of thing. But a real extremist, an ideologue, is different. The ones who *absolutely know they're right* . . . once they've tasted power, why, they'll almost *kill* to keep it. Here in Dustin — "

"Wait," my mother said, maybe just to break the flow. When Dori's dad gets on his soapbox, he can give you the impression that he'll never stop until you go to bed, or die. "I agree with you that Gabe has made himself unpopular with Dr. Leeds and other people in town who think the way that he does. I also think, both as his mother and as" — her tone got heavily ironic — "a totally dispassionate and open-minded, trained observer, that he's been ethically and legally correct in everything he's done. Craig and I are proud of him." I overdid an aw-shucks look, but I was thrilled to hear her say that. "But you admit you haven't any proof of what you just suggested. And, to be completely honest, Llew, I doubt there *is* such proof. Because I don't think anyone in town would risk serious injury to a chi-— oops! — to a person our son's age, for just the reasons that you said."

202

"Oh, I don't know," I said. "I'm not so sure of that. Those ladies who were searching cars for beer and stuff? One of them was saying what her husband said he'd do to me, if I was his. And I bet you Ronnie'd take a punch at me for under twenty bucks."

"Boy!" my father said. "My son, the kid celebrity. What's wrong with *me*? How come *I* never feel like slugging you? Is it because I voted for McGovern, do you think?" He turned to Mr. Fabb. "I'm less convinced than Pattie, Llew, when it comes to what some people here in town are capable of. But I'm also less convinced than *you* that Gabe was made a target at that program. He's told us what he called that Guardsman — strictly as a joke, *he* thought — and it *was* the sort of thing that's gotten faces punched before. That kid in uniform was still a kid, remember. They don't choose them for their judgment and cool-headedness, let's face it."

Llewellyn Fabb tried on a ghoulish smile and shook his head.

"Dustin is a lawless town, Craig. At the moment, it's a *very* lawless town," he said. "What's happening is like a western movie. You know the kind where there's this one big rich guy who completely runs the town, from the sheriff's office down? And the decent folks all look the other way? Except in Dustin there is, like, a small extremist cadre that's in power; there isn't any one guy with a thin cigar. Gabe, here, he's the cub reporter — the kid who tries to open people's eyes to what is really going on. He gets beaten, for his trouble — beaten up. The people look the other way. They are still self-righteous, or perhaps reluctant to make waves, disturb a status quo in which they're doing fine."

Llewellyn Fabb got up again. His voice had started sounding kind of dreamy.

"What this town needs," he said, "is that legendary stranger, all in black, who comes riding in, alone. A man who has the courage and a plan to open people's eyes, somehow. To stop what's happening, and make things *right*, again."

And with that he simply wandered off — down the little hall and out the door, with no good-byes for anyone. Exit Mr. Mood Swings, sure enough.

That afternoon, our copy of the *Dustin Times* arrived as usual, courtesy of Andy Bleeker, carrier and caster of that gem of local journalism. By then, my mom had long since gone to work, so there were just the two of us to tussle over who got what to read first. The riot in the high school auditorium was front page news (the headline: *Dustin H.S. Melee; Fourteen Hurt* — the subhead: *Patriotic Program Is Disrupted*). And it was also the subject of the lead, and only, editorial. Its title: *Is Something Rotten In The State Of Dustin?*

Both the news story and the editorial did a pretty good job of waffling, I'd say. In fact, I'd defy anyone to tell me who the *Dustin Times* believed was most to blame for what had happened, based on those two articles. Maybe some people would call that "careful and objective reporting," but to me it was your basic better-not-offend-them crock.

204

Example: Neither item laid a glove on D.R. Orrifice, or on whoever had invited him, to start with. In fact, and to the contrary, the congressman was credited with "a moving defense of old-fashioned patriotism" in the editorial, which also said he was "the producer of, and principal player in, a program which made plain, more clearly than a score of civics classes, the differences between our system and the Soviets'." It seems that no one told the *Times*'s reporters or its editors — none of whom was present at the scene, judging by the number of sentences that included the words "eyewitnesses reported" — about the Orrifice *v.* Morehead shoving/shouting match. Or perhaps they *were* told and didn't find it "newsworthy."

My name was in the news account, though in the editorial I was anonymous, just "the arrested student." This is from page one, verbatim:

> *At that point, Guardsmen tried to make a mock-arrest of Gabriel Podesta, 16, a junior at the high school. A scuffle ensued which, eyewitnesses reported, was shortly joined by a number of students and staff and by other members of the military. Pushing, shoving and punching soon became general, throughout the auditorium, and a number of students, faculty and soldiers suffered minor injuries before order could be restored. Fourteen people, including Mr. Podesta and nine other students, were treated and released at a first aid station established in the Nurse's Office at the school.*

"Huh? *Mister* Podesta?" my father said, when he read that. "That's perfectly ridiculous. As you know, I wasn't even *in* the high school, yesterday."

The editorial, in line with its dark title, *did* go so far as to suggest that some sort of investigation was possibly in order.

"The fact," it said, "that members of the Dustin H.S. faculty were among the first to come to the 'arrested' student's assistance suggests that eyewitness reports of excessive zeal on the part of the Guardsmen may not be exaggerated."

But this same writer also said: "Still, it does seem strange to us that a program which, Congressman Orrifice's office informed us, has been received enthusiastically and without incident in four other high schools in the district should provoke this level of reaction here in Dustin. Is it "us," or "them"? we possibly should ask ourselves. This is the second major incident inside the walls of Dustin High this term. And it's the third time there has been a confrontation that our kids have been involved in. Before 'the barrel' in the adage ends up 'spoiled,' perhaps we'd better find out who the 'rotten apples' are, and get them out of it."

Dori made it to the house about a half an hour after we were done digesting that. She accepted tea and cherry pie with chocolate ice cream from our list of daily specials, and then gave the two of us the word — as spoken down at DHS, at any rate.

"You can't *believe* the war stories," she said. "Except of course you can. Believe they're being told, I mean." She gorilla-ed out her arms and made her voice real deep and dumb. " 'So me'n Greiderman said fuck this shit — right, Greids? — if Ratsy can, then we can, too. So what we did was jump this pair of soldier-boys down by the stage, and Greids, he. . . .' " She went back to talking regular. "You can just imagine it, I'm sure."

And she balanced a big blob of melting ice cream on top of a cut-off piece of pie, then jabbed a fork through both of them and whipped 'em in her mouth before they either dripped or fell apart. She *is* an athlete, Dorinda — or maybe it's pure luck.

"But were a *lot* of people hurt?" my father asked. "The paper said fourteen, which seems like quite a few, but still, from what Gabe said. . . ."

Dori finished chewing, swallowed. "There were probably lots more that got hurt *some*," she said, "but I don't think there were any broken bones or stuff like that. A lot of people were sort of *exhibiting* their wounds — you know how they do." I looked a little quizzical, confounded. "The old red-badge-of-courage bit. I wouldn't be surprised if some of them were . . . whachacallit, *self-inflicted*, isn't it? Everybody *claims* that they were right there, in the thick of it. For one day in its life, the auditorium was *in*, the place to be." And she took another gobble.

"How about blame?" I wanted to know. "Who's taking any heat for this — not just what happened, but the whole fiasco? I mean, everybody sees it was a bum idea now, right?" I got up as I asked that, sauntered casually to the fridge and opened it. I looked inside, and then I closed it up, and after that I sauntered back and took my seat again.

"I think that's going pretty much the way that

you'd expect," she said. "Anyone with any sense thinks Orrifice is a total jerk. For the way he twisted up a perfectly good value. For the way he lost control of everything. For not seeing that it could happen, in the first place. But of course you've also got the ones who say that while he may be a bit of a dweeb, he knows what he's talking about. They use the old" — her dumb voice, again — " 'he's-a-hell-of-a-lot-smarter-than-you-are,-buddy' argument."

"So, as far as the actual *rioting* is concerned — who do they think caused *that*?" my father asked. (Bless you, father — thought his son.) "I mean, the program may have been the basic overall cause, but who's responsible, specifically? According to the person-on-the-street at DHS?"

Dori smiled. I know she knew exactly what we'd both been trying to get at.

"Well," she said, "as far as the riot's concerned, almost everybody says they think it was the *soldiers'* fault. I guess enough people saw what that guy did to Gabe. And even if they didn't, they believe what Varney's telling everybody. Varney's quite the hero, actually — "

"As indeed he should be," I broke in to say. "If he hadn't stuck his symptoms in there when he did, my cause was looking pretty hopeless, I can tell you that much." And then, for Dori's sake and so's not to waste the practice I'd put in, I rubbed my neck and grimaced. Which *did* cause her to look at me with pity and affection, both — just as many, many others would have if I'd been down there at the school all day.

"Of course," she added, "there are those who say

that Gabe provoked the soldier — *challenged* him, one person said. But then" — she shrugged — "I guess you're always going to have your G. Podesta haters. I suppose it's understandable."

Hmmm, I thought. Had I misread the look she'd given me before? Had the "pity" in it been as in "You're just so pitiful"?

"Oh, sure," I said, with practiced bitterness. "A prophet is not without honor, save in his own high school. Everyone knows that."

The phone rang; fine with me, again. My father rose to answer it. Here is what we heard:

"Yes? . . . Oh, Mr. *Morehead*! . . . No, he's *pretty* well, I'd say. He took a very hard blow to the neck, you know — as well as the punch that knocked his wind out. And, as I'm sure you realize, one doesn't want to take any chances with a neck injury. . . . Yes, I certainly will — and we ought to know more in a few days. . . . Uh-huh. Uh-huh. But while I've got you on the phone . . . let me ask you how a program such as that gets onto the school calendar to begin with. I mean, it seems to me that when you set up situations where . . . No, no. I didn't think it was *you*, necessarily, who . . . Oh. So Dr. *Leeds* contacted Mr. Orrifice, originally." He looked over at Dori and me, and winked. "Oh — after he'd heard about the program from a *friend*. . . . I see. . . . Well, I'd say 'over-tired' is a very charitable way of putting it. From all that I've been told, I'd say that the congressman's behavior was more like *irresponsible*. Especially once the program came apart. . . . Yes, I'm sure you did, although of course by *then* . . . Well, thanks for calling, Mr. Morehead.

No, I think he's napping, now. I'd rather not disturb him; he had kind of a rough night, poor kid. . . . Yes, I will, sir. . . . Right. . . . Good-bye."

He hung the thing up, smiling. I'd noticed that he'd turned his down-home golfer's accent off, while talking to the principal.

"Mr. Morehead sends you his re-gahds," he said to me.

"You said that I was 'napping'? Great. Now Morehead thinks that I'm a pansy as well as a feeb. Staying home from school and . . . napping, yet." I shook my head at Craig Podesta, communicating mock disgust.

"A pansy with, perchance, a touch of whiplash." C.P. grinned again, delighted with himself, for sure.

Dori giggled. "Keep him out on Monday, too," she said. She picked up her plate, tilted it, and proceeded to lick it clean. "That'll mean that even after three days of napping — today, tomorrow and Sunday — he still isn't all better. Morehead will have kittens. In fact, I bet right now he's on the phone with Mr. Jamison, trying to find out if he's legally responsible, as principal, or whether it's the town, the school directors, Dr. Leeds, or who!"

"Good for his digestion," C. Podesta said, inanely. "Let him bite the bullet, feel the apple, chew the nails and spit out rusty cotton. Let him hear the Muzak while on hold." He smiled and winked at us again, and patted his lean belly with both hands, the way a fat man does, sometimes.

"Tahm he started takin' better care of mah young boy," he said. And Dori, playing perfect stooge-y audience (for him), as usual, just howled.

28
SATURDAY

The next day, Saturday, was . . . oh, let's hide behind "remarkable"; that's "interesting," but more so. No, I didn't nap at all. And no one "kept" me out of school, except the genius who invented Saturdays, and all the precious freedoms that go with them. If I were ever given the job of making up a coat of arms for Saturday, I'd have to find out what the Latin is for "you don't have to." I wouldn't do that on a Saturday, of course.

As usual, I got up late. Saturdays are about the same length as regular days for most of the people I know; the only difference is we take some up-time off the top of them and add it to the bottom. So it was more or less eleven when I saw how nice it was inside the dome and got the radio to tell me that it might be even nicer elsewhere.

I called up Dori and remarked upon that fact. She said she'd noticed and already had a plan to put before me. Wouldn't it be the perfect day for us, "the three of us," to climb Everly Mt.?

"Hmmm," I said, judiciously, a little disappointed. "Isn't there a saying? 'Two's company, but three's a — ' "

"You, me and a picnic lunch," she clarified.

"Good crowd," I answered instantly. Much as I enjoy Lafountain, there are times I'd rather have a picnic lunch around, lunchtime being only one example.

I said I'd see if I could get my mother's car; I'd call her back. And also, what about that night? (I asked.) Had she another plan already on the drawing board, a lecture we could go to, maybe? Something with a patriotic theme, perhaps?

"Well," she said, "my father says he has to go to the Jettison City library today, to see about some exhibit that they want to get for here, and he thought that while he was there, he might have dinner with his cousin Justin, which'd mean he wouldn't get back here till really, really late. But seeing as you hadn't mentioned doing anything, I sort of said I'd go to Arby Fremont's party — I think he said his parents were away this weekend. Deano told me it was going to have a Spanish theme; he said it was an *Olé* Party. But then I found it was an *Oil* of Olay party, and I've no idea what *that* means" — she gave a little giggle — "so I guess I'll have to wait and see. However, if you know a lecture we could go to . . . well, I think I'd like that, too. I mean, the last one that we went to was a riot. . . ."

212

"Or, how about we rent a movie and you spend the night?" I said sincerely, *urgently*, in fact. Dori likes to keep me on my toes (I think) by *pretending* (I believe) that she might do something idiotic, like going to one of Arby Fremont's "parties." I am grateful to her. Staying on one's toes builds up the muscles in one's calves.

"Okay," she said, at once. She's not a meanie. "And you'll call me back about the car?"

"ASAP," I said, and went to look for someone in authority.

It was my father who I found available; Mom was on the telephone. He said that sounded like a great idea, a picnic did — almost *too* great for a lad who maybe should be napping — but that, yes, I could have access to the Subaru. He would let my mother drive the "Bug" in an emergency. He also said there'd been a lot of calls, that morning.

"Uh-oh," I said. "I hope they weren't really gross. You ought to just hang up, you know. That's what it says to do in the phone directory. They say it's better to hang up, and not talk back, or show them that you're angry or upset. You see those people get — "

"These weren't heavy-breather types," my father said. "In fact, amazingly, they've all been very sympathetic. People asking how you *were*, saying it's a *shame* the whole thing ever *happened*, how you ought to get a *medal* or perhaps a ticker tape *parade* — you know the type of thing."

"*That* call," said my mother, who'd hung up while we were talking, "was from Mrs. Gratz. She wanted to know how they expected her to teach Eddie values like Respect for Law when they bring in speakers telling him it's okay if certain people break it."

"And what did *you* say, fount of wisdom?" asked my father.

She said, "I said, 'Why bless Ed Senior's fuzz-buster, *I* sure don't know.' " She laughed.

"You *are* a wiseass," said my father. "But, *touché*."

"No," she said. "Dorothy's all right. We kid around. She knows I like both her and Ed. She calls me Mrs. . . . what's-his-name, *you* know, the guy that started Summerhill?"

"Neill," my father said. "And speaking of per-missiveness, I told *mah* boy that he could have *your* car, today — to take that sweet Dorinda on a picnic. I wasn't going to, but I thought: Well, shoot; she maybe saved his *life*. Seems like we owe her *some-thing*. They gonna climb Everly Mt."

"Fair enough," my mother said, and turned to me. "Invite her back for dinner and the night, why don't you? That ought to even up the score — or maybe put us just a little bit ahead; we're having leg of lamb. Or, wait, we're not. I clean forgot. The master of the house and I are going *out* to dinner."

"Right," I said. "I will. Invite her. In fact, I have, already. We can cook something for ourselves. She said her father would be gone again, till real, real late."

"Ah, so?" my mother said. She pursed her lips, then tightened them a little, shook her head. I'm pretty sure she'd just as soon have Dori *live* with us, full time — if it hadn't been for all the reasons that made that a poor idea. I know she would have liked to have another female in the house, at times, es-

214

pecially a specimen she liked that much.

I left a short while later, and picked Dorinda up, and drove the thirty-five or forty miles to Everly. It's not a mountain everybody's heard of, though a lot more folks have heard of it than climbed it. It's in a rural section of the state and off the beaten track. There aren't any roads or trails on it, except for remnants from the last time it was logged, and new ones made by animals. But there are some pretty great long views, when you look south from near the top. On the mountain's north side there's this area they call "the oven," where it looks as if someone with a giant butterknife took a big whack at the mountainside, and went away with a bunch of it, leaving just a concave, real steep slope. I think it's much too steep to ski down, but the steepness helps the view. And at one time or another, first with my parents and later with Dori and Lafountain, I've climbed most of it — although without the style and expertise of someone like a Varney Poole. It was just a real nice, rugged, little mountain, or big hill, part of one long, wooded ridge, twenty-seven-hundred-eighty feet in height, the maps all said.

Because we'd breakfasted so late, it just made common sense to lug our picnic to the top and eat it there. We had a favorite little knob we liked, an open, rocky space where you could sit and see down into White Creek valley, with Bear Mt. on the other side of it. And looking west, you probably could see — oh, I don't know — at least a hundred *other* miles of beautiful terrain, all wooded hills and mountains and the drop-offs in between. You don't see any evidence of *people* from up there, unless you see

215

a car on that one road in White Creek valley. You're simply looking at this most amazing Earth of ours, a world so beautiful and complicated — and so *right* — that all the artists who have ever lived have not come close to dreaming up a better-looking version of the place.

That's the way it seemed to me that day, in any case, when I laid eyes on it, again. So, naturally, it's what I said to Dori, with my mouth part full of peanut butter-bacon sandwich, and a cup of grape juice mixed with ginger ale in hand.

"Yup," she said, "that's right. Of course it helps we're far enough away so we can't see a lot of details. The different little beasties beating one another up, down there."

Women are such realists, so unromantic, sometimes. On top of that: They often are correct. But I wasn't going to let this fang-and-claw talk change my mood. So I agreed with her, and more.

"*Eating* one another up," I said, and waved my sandwich at her. "All the world's a high school, as I think I said to Dr. Leeds, one time."

"Oh, it may not be *that* bad," she said, perversely. And then, "Although one *can* come up with similarities. For instance: lots of different kinds of fungus, vegetables and plants, pecking orders, predators and prey."

"Isn't it amazing that, as smart as people are compared to animals, supposedly, they don't just *stop*?" I said. "I mean, the stuff like killing. Beating one another up. Putting people down. You know, the major stinkos."

The way that I was feeling it was fun to theorize

and speculate. About Utopia, for instance. I've noticed that great views have that effect on people. They make them think of hopeful sentences, starting with "Why not . . ?", "What if . . ?", and "Isn't it amazing. . . ?"

"Or maybe it's amazing they don't totally destroy each other," Dori said. "As smart as people are."

So much for my "great views" theory. I rummaged in her pack and found another sandwich, this one simple lettuce and tomato. I realize that l & t is not a big-name sandwich, but the way that Dori makes them — salt and pepper and a ton of mayonnaise — they (soggily) excite me. Especially since I learned tomatoes are a fruit. I mean, a *fruit* sandwich? Is that Peculiar Food Experiment material, or what?

"You mean that *either* one is possible," I said. "It's up to us." I guess I knew by then our moods were not identical, but still I — stupidly — kept pushing for agreement, searching for a common ground.

Dori sighed and smiled. She might not have felt like it, but she was going to be agreeable, I was pretty sure. I think she thought that I was convalescing, still.

"Peace or war," she said. "That's the way it goes. True or false. Red or black. Up or down. Coke or Pepsi. Wanna fight about it?"

"No," I said, and put my sandwich down and reached for her. Better to shut up, I told myself. Typically, agreeably, she got right close to me, and we arranged our arms around each other, slowly sank onto a horizontal plane, nicely stretched and touching all along the length of us. I loved her just a ton, that day, no doubt about it. But even when I felt like shit, I loved her, even when I couldn't say it. Love may be the one forever feeling. I'd read that once, somewhere, and I believed it.

But there are other, passing feelings, too — connected feelings, attributes, accessories of love. And I was feeling one of them right then: *Desire!* Which feeling made me think that *this* might be a *most* fantastic time to *do* it! Check out the scenario: Naked in the sunshine on a mountaintop? What could be more right, more *natural*? And, too, remember this: I could have been killed *dead*, two days before! What better way was there to shout "I am ALIVE! I'm not the least bit DEAD!" than *doing* it?

I flopped around with that idea a while. I guess the word is "fantasized." It was pleasant; she was gorgeous; I was great; she loved it, so did I (guys always do). We changed positions, stimulated old locations newly, wallowed in each other's appetites, made repeated use of words like "just the greatest." *Marveled* at one partner's stamina, control. Oh, yeah; oh, yeah; oh, yeah, yeah, yeah.

That was the fantasy. The facts, of course, were otherwise. You guessed? You're right. It really *wasn't* time for us, again. For reasons old and new, the new including Dori's present mood. I was surely up, but she seemed slightly off, a little down. When the time *was* right, we'd both be up, sky high.

Up and down, I mused. Our moods — yes, everybody's moods — are changing constantly from up to down and back again — and often pausing in between. Love goes on and on, but so does *change* (I thought). Amazing. What else does? Go on and on, I mean. I couldn't think of anything. That seemed peculiar. Were love and change the only constants in the universe? And does that mean there is a God? It seemed to me it did. I thought that was a fragile and elusive understanding — not the sort of thing you'd tell Lafountain.

I also thought that, well, in spite of everything and all conclusions drawn and all decisions reached, I wanted to be up again, or maybe partly, still. Some good could come of that. And so, in hopes of one thing leading to another (how I hate admitting junk like this!), I got my head and Dori's head in place so I could kiss her.

"The trouble with my father," Dori said, before I had our lips together, "is he *may* think only one is possible."

"What?" I said. "One what?" I hadn't planned for her to talk. On the page I'd hoped for us to end up on, there wasn't any talk at all, just panting sounds.

"One *outcome*," she replied. "One possibility. He may think it's *always* Coke. Or Pepsi."

"Right," I said. Except it wasn't right at all. Things seemed all jumbled in my head. Shit, I thought, I didn't know where Dori's father stood on soft drinks *or* on possibilities. He didn't even seem to have moods, other than spacey, or hyper. Those were the ones that he changed back and forth between, both "downs." I'd never heard him say anything that suggested he saw any possibility of anything getting any better.

"I don't think he *believes* in hoping," Dori said. "Sometimes I think he doesn't even *want* things to get better. If they did, that'd sort of take away the main thing in his life, dwelling on how rotten things and people are."

I tried to think that over. "I don't know," I said. But what I thought I *did* know was that any possibility of "up" had just gone out the window. She had seized the reins and turned the horse around; we were heading in the opposite direction. Her father, as a subject or a person, was a "down." I'd heard my mother talk about depression some, the chronic kind that people get and can't get out of, or not without some expert help. It looked to me as if the guy had that. What had to happen, somehow, was that he get diagnosed. Know what the trouble is, and you can start to fix it — revelation by Podesta, G. But useless, lacking Llew-llew Fabb's cooperation.

"I just don't know," I said again. "I just wish he'd go and see my mother."

As I said that, I disentwined and struggled to my feet. No question, now my mood had swung, and I was feeling quite distinctly crabby. I wished that Dori hadn't brought her father up. I would have wished that even if I hadn't had my own agenda on my mind. I knew she worried constantly about the guy, but still. Couldn't we have a few hours when we didn't go round and round about whatever he'd been doing lately, or his overall condition? I mean, on this one day, just two days after I'd been beaten up (and, luckily, not worse), couldn't we have bagged that dreary and depressing subject?

Pretty soon, we started down. I found it almost laughable (oh, ha-ha-ha) the way I couldn't just reach out and get my old mood back. Pathetic. Hell, I was a guy who *knew* things changed, why not just point myself in that direction and proceed to lighten up? What was the point of knowing stuff you couldn't *use?*

We followed what had always been our favorite brook as it took tumbles down the mountain. When we passed its deepest little pool, Dori double-dared me to go skinny-dipping in it, with herself for company. She swore she would, if I did. I almost got myself to do it, too, imagining how that might be, both of us as bare as babies, but much different, naturally, and *naturally* inclined to. . . . Then my crabbiness kicked in again and made me actually *not want to*, and I grunted out some line like "Hell-we'd-freeze-our-butts," or something just as wonderfully original.

And when I thought about that, driving home, it made me feel even worse.

When we were getting ready to pass by the place we'd come to more or less a month before, when Dori'd gotten me to drive her out of town, and we had stood there in the drizzle, looking at the river, Dori said, "Hey, pull on over here, all right?"

I'm pretty sure I sighed, just like this almost total jerk that I'd become. But also I pulled over, stopped the car.

"Gabe. What's the matter?" Dori said. And that was all the stimulus I needed.

Eyes closed and blindly reaching out, I dived in her direction, absolutely bawling, sobbing from my heart, almost hysterical.

She held my head against her chest and said, "Oh, Gabe. Poor Gabe," and so she let me have the feel-

221

ings that I hadn't known were there until they'd come and overwhelmed me.

"Everything is such a *mess*," I kept on saying, meaning surely me and all the things I wasn't, maybe never would be, and the high school and the town, and ups and downs, her father, and this whole confusing planet.

Dori just said, "Yes, I know," and kind of patted me and nuzzled me and rocked me. She didn't contradict me or deny me anything; instead she just stayed with me, where I was, and just because she could, and did, she told me in a new way that she loved me.

In maybe half an hour I was fine. Well, I don't know about *fine*, but at least no longer just a sodden blob, a basket case. I felt exhausted, ready for a nap, but also strangely purified, as if I'd gotten over a disease and now could start to build back up to normal.

Here's something funny. I really didn't think I'd acted like a jerk, but still I had to say I had, that I was sorry. Dori only looked at me, her eyes all huge and tender, her lips just slightly parted, as if about to smile. I never will forget that look, not ever, not forever.

Back at the house, I thought I got some different kinds of looks from both my parents, which made me wonder if my eyes were red, or shifty. My father also said I'd had a call from Jim Colangelo, the cop. No message, just would I call back? He handed me the number, scrawled on one of his prescription pads; he was, of course, "The Putting Doctor." I went into the den and dialed.

"Oh, yeah," Jim said, when I'd admitted who it was. "So, how you doing, Gabe? . . . That's good, real good. I heard you took a few good raps. . . . Well, look, the reason that I called is . . . this is kind of complicated, but. . . ."

It wasn't all that *complicated*. Pretty rotten, yes, a little bit surprising and depressing, slightly upbeat at the end. Not really all that complicated, though.

Seems Jim had a buddy, Murray Slater — I remembered him, the shortstop — who was in the same battalion, or whatever, as the guys who traveled with the congressman and dressed as Russian soldiers. Murray'd heard the story from those guys, that day, from the ones who'd been at Dustin High and in the riot and now were out at camp, that weekend. And he'd called up Jim to tell him all about it, knowing he'd be interested.

Dori's father had been right, apparently. I *had* been fingered. The Guardsmen had been told there were some real jerks in our school. Losers with an attitude about America, the flag, the President, and so on. Wiseguys everybody else in school would love to see, like, taught a little lesson. So, if the opportunity arose . . . (Murray wasn't sure; there might have been some signal from the congressman) . . . the troops were told the students and the faculty would cheer, and maybe even get a few licks in, themselves. Of course, they were amazed and shocked when tons of people seemed to rush to my defense.

Later on, some officers got wind of all that happened and began to raise some holy hell about it. Murray'd said the guy who hit me, first . . . he said his ass was really in a sling.

"Good," I said. "Anything he gets is fine with me. Anyone who'd do a thing like that — beat up a poor defenseless kid he didn't even know." I made a little joke of it, but I was serious.

"Murray said he wasn't anybody special," Jim replied. "Just a guy who thought he was doing the right thing at the time. Sticking up for the country, I guess." He gave a nervous-sounding laugh when he said that.

We talked a little longer, and I got the feeling Jim felt very bad that this had happened, *embarrassed* that a person in a uniform would break the law like that. He told me that he'd heard a lot of people on the *force* — as well as regular civilians — stick up for me and say that they admired how I had the guts to say what I believed, no matter what.

"Hell," he said, and laughed again, "there's even people starting to *agree* with you. Before you know it, they'll be wanting *you* for school director, Gabe."

"Sure," I said. "Oh, sure." But I was grateful to the guy. He hadn't had to call — or say that. "Thanks a million, Jim. I really do appreciate your calling."

"Well, I thought you ought to know that it's been taken care of. You hang in there, Gabe," he said. "So long."

I went into the living room and told the story to my parents and Dorinda. Their reactions were about the same as mine. Nobody mentioned that Llewellyn Fabb had been quite right, for once, in his suspicions.

"I guess," my father said, "this makes it pretty clear that Dr. Leeds is *the* main sickie in the picture. You know, the guy with his forked fingers sticking up behind the head of sanity, in town. . . ."

Imagining him doing that actually made me laugh. My mother said she thought his days were numbered as a school director; Dori and yours truly said we'd eat to that. And so, when they went over to their friends' for dinner, the two of us stuffed face with burgers, fries and salad, followed by some Sara Lee concoction and an entertainment by the brothers Marx. Don't tell the members of our union (High School Swingers, Local 48), but both of us were fast asleep in separate beds before eleven. And on a Saturday, no less.

29
GLOOMY SUNDAY

The next day, Sunday, was a loser when it came to looks. Dark — and doubtless raining, out from under. I saw that as soon as I got up, at a respectable but hardly crack-of-dawn-ish hour; ten A.M. I used an "-ish" word there to show you that I'm not afraid to wield expressions that my mother doesn't like. But still, I didn't call the meal Lafountain soon would serve himself, and spill a little of upon the kitchen table, "brunch." It wasn't that much trouble to say "breakfast": It was just one extra syllable.

"Lafountain called last night," I told my mom as I began to line up oranges to squeeze. "He said that he'd invited Varney Poole for breakfast. Here. To-day. He also asked me if I thought you'd mind, to be completely fair."

"And what did *you* say?" asked the matriarch *pro*

tem. Her partner in all this had not yet risen.

"I said I didn't think you would, unless you hadn't eaten first," I said. "That maybe you'd be glad he had. But I reminded Lafountain that once this year's maple syrup crop is used up, there won't be any more until next spring. And had he thought about the possible effect our having Varney here might have on *his* own Sunday breakfasts, between now and then."

"And what did he say to *that*?" the maternal ancestor inquired.

"He said good grief he *hadn't* thought of that," I said. "He called himself a dunderhead. And worse. He said he wondered if he had a self-destructive streak he'd been repressing. You know how much Lafountain loves his syrup. Or *our* syrup, as it happens. I've heard him say he'd eat a *brussels sprout* with maple syrup on it."

"Well," my mother said, "that's pretty extreme. But, despite the dangers, I'm still glad we're having Varney over. In fact, I'm going to lie and tell him I *told* Lafountain to invite him. That way, there won't be any confusion about who Varney should be the most grateful to. But do you think we've got enough butter? Should I pick up another firkin or two? Or another sack of flour? A few dozen extra eggs? Oh, hi, Dori," she added, as D. Fabb came clomping in. "Sleep well? Were the towels fluffy enough? Say 'Yes' to both of those and we'll be almost even."

"Huh?" asked Dori, looking like the word itself. She doesn't wake up with all pistons firing.

"Mom's still on her little payback project," I explained. "It's her crude way of saying thank you to the people in the auditorium who helped her only son survive. You should have got a leg of lamb, last night. Varney's coming for the hash and eggs and pancakes. I can't decide whether to be flattered or hurt. I mean, it isn't every day you get to hear your value in commodities and services and stuff."

"Um," said Dori, pouring herself a glass of cider and not even trying to get it. "Well, I'm just going to wake up a little and then go over to the house. Maybe I'll stick around and say hi to Varney and Lafountain, though. If my dad was all that late, he won't be getting up before noon. Oh — and promise you won't even *think* of driving me. I'd rather walk, no kidding."

"Okey-doke," I said, and started squeezing o's.

Pretty soon, my father made the scene and got the coffee going. Then he opened cans of hash and dumped them in our biggest bowl, which he'd put down on the counter in front of the cabinet with all the different spices and condiments in it. Then, making his usual display of secretiveness, he proceeded to take down various jars and bottles and to shake them over the bowl. We never got to see which ones were part of his "secret seasonings," of course, or whether he actually took the tops off before he did the shaking. But when he was done, he made a great show of mixing everything together with his hands. My mother sometimes made a comment at this point that related, I believe, to his psychological development in early childhood, but it's much too gross for me to pass along. At least in English — and I can't come up with all the words in Spanish.

I, meanwhile, made up a big batch of pancake batter and poured some syrup into a pitcher. Dori's morning fog cleared up enough for her to set the table. And, at eleven sharp, Lafountain had his appetite right where it belonged, on our back doorstep. Varney had some trouble with the traffic, coming over; he didn't ring the front doorbell until two minutes past the hour.

For most of everyone's first helping, we talked and joked about the riot, pretty much as if the thing had been a . . . joke. You know how it gets after something serious has been over for a little while and nobody in the room has been — or will be — seriously affected by whatever happened. People tend to goof around, even when they're saying something that means a great deal to them, like in the case of my parents and their "thanks a lot for helping Buster-Bob," to Varney. They're apt to call me by a lot of different names, depending.

Varney, on his part, insisted that he probably would never have left his seat if he'd thought about it first. He also tried to tell us that the only reason he'd grabbed the soldier who'd hit me was for the guy's own sake.

"If I hadn't, Dori might have got to him," he said, "with results too awful to imagine." Lafountain, piling it on, said that with a few good men like Varney under his command, he could pretty much guarantee an end to terroristic acts in Lebanon, and probably a new hit sitcom.

"Oh, speaking of that kind of thing," said Varney, then, "there's a movement starting in the social studies department down at school to recall Dr. Leeds."

"Re*call*?" said Lafountain. "What, they can't remember him from Thursday? Tall, skinny dude up on the platform? Just the one weird earring?"

"No, no," said Varney. "Not re*call*, *re*-call. It's like impeachment, sort of. *Re*-call's where some person, some official like a school director, gets removed from office by a special vote. Some people in the department are starting a petition, from what I understand. And I heard that several of the department chairpersons went to Morehead Friday with the same idea in mind. They want that doctor *out* of there."

"Well, me, I've got to get me out of *here*," said Dori, standing up. "So long, you guys. And thanks a lot, Mr. and Mrs. Podesta. I really think you've more than paid me back. The towels were *super*-fluffy, and I even think the bathroom scale is light a pound or two. I'll call you later, Gaberoo."

With that, she waved and left, never one to drag an exit out. In the momentary pause in the conversation that so often comes when someone goes, Varney and Lafountain both restocked their plates, refilled their cups, and smiled at one another. I don't think either of them had thought of Dori as any sort of competitor in the eat-a-thon that they'd embarked on, but they probably agreed that it was nice to have one fewer person fussing with the food supply.

My parents were interested in what Varney'd said about Leeds being ousted from office, so that subject was considered further, then. And of course everybody wondered if T. Hank and Mrs. Teagle would stay on in the absence of their spiritual leader. We also mused about replacements for the gang of three.

230

Varney told my mother that she ought to run, but she demurred.

"It wouldn't be smart politics," she said. "Getting rid of Leeds would be a major plus, a real accomplishment. But if I ran it might be seen as trying to rub it in." She looked across the table at my father, and she smiled. "Craig would be a better choice. A man who drives a white Bugatti ought to be electable in Dustin, don't you think? He's in the fast lane, true, but always to the right of center."

"You know, I just *might* run," my father said. He smiled his goofy smile, but I thought that he was serious. My father likes to do the unexpected, to learn a lot of different ways to sink whatever putts might come his way in life. Now, he opened up the *Sunday Magazine* and started on the crossword puzzle, working from the lower right-hand corner up, this time.

Others of us picked up other sections of the paper, too, and offered one another shrewd and trenchant observations and opinions on such diverse subjects as Rickie Natiel, Elliott Abrams, Milo's Meadow, computer-generated art, Bruce Willis's general style and Senator Bradley of New Jersey. There weren't any "undecideds" on those topics, but when Lafountain asked Varney and me if we'd rather be stranded on a desert island with an unlimited supply of (a) hash and eggs, (b) pancakes and syrup or (c) Greta Scacchi, a lack of certainty, of strong commitment, was apparent right away. As our analysis grew deeper and more complicated, and we started to get into related issues such as tooth decay and the companionship potential of protein (as compared to complex carbohydrates), my father sighed and rose to wash a bunch of plates and cups. But shortly after that, Varney and Lafountain found a couple of bags of apples that they'd somehow missed before, and so they went and got their plates again, so they could slice and set Macoun and McIntosh against each other, based on texture, juiciness and eye-appeal, as well as what Lafountain called "the tang of autumn." My father sighed again, and went back to his puzzle, now three-quarters done.

It wasn't long after that that Dori came back. I was at the sink by then, finishing the pots and pans. The rest of the group was still at the table, now playing team Sorry (if you know that board game), my parents against the other two. I guess no one paid much heed to D's return, at first. She wasn't expected, but she wasn't *un*expected, either. And she'd been there — what? — an hour and a half or so, before. What I'm saying is there didn't seem to be a need, or reason, to react to her arrival. But as I shut the water off and turned around, I heard the way she said that first word: "Please . . . " And right away I knew there *was* a reason, and that something terrible had happened.

"*Please*," she said again, a little louder. "I think I need some help. My father isn't home. He has been, but he left. There was this note, here, on the kitchen table."

She had a folded piece of paper in her hand, which she then gave to my mother. My mother opened it and laid it on our kitchen table, between my father and herself. I naturally went over, bent and peered between their heads at it.

232

The note was done in pen, and it was written in an ugly and irregular, and childlike, hand. Those words can also be applied to my own writing, but his, unlike my own, was very legible. Here is what it said:

Dori dearest,

You must go out of town. Make Gabe and his parents take you and stay with you somewhere, for overnight. Don't think about it, only go, at once. It's the first and only favor I will ever ask.

What I intend to do is something I must do alone — I could not do it well with thee. I am not afraid or worried. I give no importance to what happens to myself.

Part of me is always with thee, Dori, so there's no good-bye.

Love forever,
Dad

As soon as I had read it I went over to her.

"Oh, Gabe," she said. "I think he's going to kill himself."

Naturally, I wrapped my arms around her, and she dropped her head against the inside of my shoulder, gulping. Behind me, I could hear my parents talking in low tones. Varney and Lafountain had got up and come around the table so's to read the note themselves. I heard old Varney say, "Why 'thee'? Is Mr. Fabb a Quaker?"

Almost automatically, I turned my head and answered him, still clutching Dori. It was as if I'd known the answer all along and didn't even have to think about it.

"No," I said, "no, no. That isn't him. That's Robert Jordan talking. The guy in *For Whom the Bell Tolls*? A lot of that's right from the novel; I'm really pretty sure. When I was at the library, he mentioned Robert Jordan — except that *I* thought he was saying *Michael* Jordan, dope — and he had the book right there, right on his desk." I moved my head, looked down at Dori.

"Those other books you said that he'd been reading?" I went on. "The ones about explosives? And the trips that he's been taking? This note must mean he's going to, maybe . . . well. . . ."

She'd lifted up her face while I was talking.

"Yes," she said. "Blow up the dome. He'd think that that was what he had to do, to help the town. Change it back to how it used to be. And he *wouldn't* care what happened to himself — or anybody else, except for me and you guys."

As she said that last, she looked at me, and then at both my parents, and at Varney and Lafountain right behind them. Absurdly, the thought popped into my mind that Varney and Lafountain had just lucked out by being there, that Mr. Fabb hadn't mentioned *them* in his note, and probably didn't care one way or the other whether they were hit by falling sky, or not. But Dori, looking at my parents, spoke again.

234

"What should I *do*?" she said. "Do you think I ought to call the cops, or what?"

I looked at my parents, too. Although I'd been the one who gave that explanation of the note, I wanted them to tell me it was crazy, wrong, *impossible*. I wanted them to tell the bunch of us the note meant something else, that Mr. Fabb could not be that screwed up, no way.

Instead, they started asking questions. Not about Robert Jordan, the American who'd taken on the job of blowing up a bridge in Spain; they'd both read Hemingway and knew about that guy, already. No, they wanted more about Llewellyn Fabb and this interest of his in blowing up buildings or whatever, and whether Dori'd ever seen anything around her house in the way of high explosives, wires, detonators, or what have you. Don't forget, they'd *heard* him talk about the town, and about how it needed some lone stranger with a plan, someone to ride on in and make things right again. But what they'd never heard — which I had — was Mr. Fabb maintaining that the dome was the cause of all the changes in the town. Or at least the ones he didn't like.

Dori couldn't tell them much, but she did tell them *that* — about his thing about the dome. She said she hadn't seen any suspicious-looking boxes or anything, but she also said she hadn't been in the garage for months. She told them what she could about the books, and how her father had explained his interest in them. Everything she said did not take long.

When she was done, my parents looked at one another.

235

"I think we ought to go to the police," my father said. He seemed to address us all, as a group. "*I* ought to go, at least; I'm pretty friendly with a few of them. And maybe all the rest of you should, well, get out of town." He looked back at my mother. "You could all go to Vivian and Tony's." That was my aunt and uncle's place, a big house in the country, outside of Rumbard, maybe forty miles away. Tony was my mother's brother.

Then he added, "Wait. I'm being stupid." He looked at Varney and Lafountain. "You both have people that you'd want to . . . tell. Of course. You've got your car," he said to Varney. "And I can swing on by Lafountain's house on my way to the station."

"I'm going to try to find Llew," my mother said. "Maybe I can talk him out of this . . . whatever he's got planned. He came to see me down at work last week; we have . . . like, a relationship. Take Gabe with you," she said to my father, "and then, after, you can take him out to Tony's. Dori, you can — "

"I'm going to go with you," she told my mother. "I can help you, can't I? I know he said for me to leave town, but — "

"I'd like to go with you, too," Varney then chimed in, also talking to my mother. "If Mr. Fabb's planning what Gabe said, that could involve some climbing, right? I've got equipment in my car. And, well, I'm not from here, remember. There isn't anybody special that I need to warn. Besides," he rubbed his chin, "I respect Mr. Fabb, the little that I know, the stuff he thinks. I'd like to try to help him. I don't mean blow up the dome," he added hastily. "*You*

236

know." Old Varney, always having trouble saying what he meant, just right.

"I think Dori ought to go with you, at first," my mother said to my father. Then she turned to Dori. "I don't believe the police would act so quickly, just on Craig's say-so. They'd want to know who found the note and what the background of it is — the kind of things that you can tell them best. And I think they should act quickly. Your father's perfectly capable of trying to destroy the dome. And there's another side to it. I wouldn't care to guess how his seeing you might affect him at this point. It might make him stop — I think it probably would — but it also might really upset him. He must be in a pretty agitated state, right now. I just don't know."

I watched Dori chew on that. It struck me that she might have thought things over, since she'd gotten here, and decided that she didn't want to stop her father, after all. That possibly she now believed that wrong or right, lunatic or visionary, he should just be let alone to take his shot. That she should do him that one favor, after all.

She didn't give away what she was thinking. Not by any look that *I* know, anyway. "All right," she said. "I'll go with Mr. Podesta, then. And after that, perhaps, he'll take me where my father is, if anyone can find him."

"Well, I guess I *ought* to go on home," Lafountain said. I'd almost forgotten he was there. "If Mr. P. could drop me, like he said. Then, maybe, afterwards. . . ." He shrugged and dropped his eyes. "We'll see."

That seemed to take care of everybody but me. I felt peculiar, torn. I thought I ought to go with Dori, be some comfort to her, maybe. That was on the one hand. But on the other . . . well, that seemed like such a small, *inactive* role. I wanted to do something *big* for Dori. The trouble was, I couldn't think of what, and nobody was helping me at all. It wasn't quite the time for letters to the editor.

"How about if Gabe, here, comes with me," said Varney, suddenly. "Us, I mean." He nodded at my mother, spoke to her, then. "It's possible I'll need another pair of hands."

I looked at Varney, grateful to the guy but having no idea what he could mean. Another pair of hands? For what? To help subdue Llewellyn Fabb — a raging mad Llewellyn Fabb — while hanging from a rope a hundred meters off the ground?

"That might not be a bad idea," my mother calmly said. "Is that all right with you?" She looked at me. "I know you'd rather be with Dori, but — "

"Go with them, Gabe," Dori said to me. "Please — *please*. I'll see you later, somewhere."

I looked at my father. He was nodding, too. It was possible that Dori was trying to keep me away from the police station, I thought. If she'd decided to be difficult, she wouldn't want me there to say the stuff I'd heard him say about the dome, and all the other Robert Jordan and explosives stuff.

"Just let me get my running shoes," I said to Varney, pointing at my slippered feet. My heart was really thumping and, for once, I didn't have another thing to say.

238

30
STANCHION PARTY (3)

Varney drives a sporty little Nissan Pulsar, red. The three of us squeezed in: Varney and my mother and myself. My mother had also made a quick change of clothes — to a warm-up suit and workout sneakers — and when I saw that I realized for the first time, I guess, that she was prepared to make a house call on Llewellyn Fabb, wherever he might be. That thought did nothing for my butterflies at all. As I think I mentioned before, those stanchions go up for some five hundred feet. Next time you see a fifty-story building, take careful note of just how high it is. Like that.

We talked. None of us had the slightest idea, of course, of how many stanchions you'd have to destroy in order to bring down the dome — *or* how much explosive you'd use on each one, *or* exactly where you'd put it, in relation to the top or bottom. From the general information files that people carry around in their heads we all pulled out some barely decipherable mental notes about "plastic" explosives being both a smaller and more stable charge to use than dynamite. And by having had the experience of driving past blasting sites and seeing signs telling you to turn off two-way radios, we'd gotten the idea that Mr. Fabb would probably set off his blasts that way, by radio, rather than by pushing a T-handle down into a black box that had a long wire coming out of it. With a wild look in his eyes, of course.

"You know," said Varney, "it's possible he started after dark, last night, and now he's almost done, and may be lying low until it's dark again. You've seen the stanchions; anyone who's not an expert climber's going to need a ladder to get up that lower part. There aren't any built-in rungs for fifty feet at least. So passersby might see the ladder and look up, and see a guy up there and maybe call the cops."

"That's right," I said, "as long as you're being completely calm and rational about the whole thing. But there's no telling how a guy like Mr. Fabb would look at it. I mean, if he thinks he's the Lone Ranger or whatever it is, it's possible he'd also think that no one *would* look up, or even come along — or if they did, they wouldn't even see him. Don't you think that's possible?" I asked my mother.

"No," she said, and sighed. She was looking pretty hyper. "I don't want to talk about Llew's mental state, but I'm pretty sure he isn't delusional enough to think that he's got special powers or protection. What he *does* think is that he can see things — circumstances or reality, let's say — much more clearly than the rest of us. Except, perhaps, for you."

"Who, *Gabe*?" said Varney, with what I'd have to say was an incredulous inflection.

"Yes, Gabe," my mother said, and I was glad to see her smile. "As odd as that may seem to us. But Llew believes that Gabe is very special. He's been very much concerned about his safety, even back before the riot. And part of that concern relates to his relationship with Dori, of course. Llew thinks the town contributed to — almost *caused* — the breakup of his marriage, and he doesn't want it to destroy his daughter's happiness as well. It's pretty complicated, his concern. And not entirely rational, of course." And then she sighed, again.

By then, the Nissan was on Roosevelt Avenue, heading for the edge of town.

"Now, where's that little road. . . ?" said Varney in a mumble. And I realized that he was heading for the stanchion where we'd held the party, weeks and weeks before.

"It's coming up, just past the cemetery there," I said, and Varney hit the blinker, turned the Nissan sharply off the road, across the jogging path, and kept on going till he reached the pilings stuck into the ground. There was another car right there already, a Buick Skylark, class of '67, with some padding on its roof.

"He's here," I said — of course unnecessarily. I couldn't help it, had to talk — say something.

Varney pointed at the Skylark's roof and said, "I'd say he brought a ladder." He sounded pretty pleased

241

to me, self-satisfied. But neither he nor my mother threw open their doors and jumped out of the car. I don't think any of us had expected to find him so quickly. I know I'd been prepared for lots of looking, driving here and there. We didn't have a plan in place.

"Hmm," said Varney. Teachers are great silence-fillers. They're all used to taking charge. I think it gets to be an automatic thing with them: When there's a silence, speak.

"I'll get out first," he said. Varney was a rookie, but he had the tone down pat; we children paid attention, got the word. "I'll get binoculars. I have some in the trunk. And then, I'll . . . I'll act a little *weird*, as if I were a bird-watcher, just in case he's watching me from someplace. What I'll do is creep off into the underbrush and after a while I'll be able to check out the stanchion from someplace where he won't be able to see me."

At that point he looked over at my mother. She was clearly not a student in his class. And so his face became entirely different. Now it was entirely interrogative, as if to say, "Does that make any sense to you?"

"Good," my mother said. "I think that's good. Gabe and I will stay right here. Take your time, act natural. But go. No, wait." She rummaged in the glove compartment, found the owner's manual and handed it to Varney. "He'll think that you've been looking in your bird book."

Varney got out and went around to the trunk of his car and opened it. A minute later, when he pulled it down, he looked a great deal different. He not

242

only had a pair of binoculars looped around his neck, but he'd also managed to mess up his hair and yank out one of his front shirttails. And as he walked away from the car, his body angled slightly forward, and he *bounced*. Another time I would have laughed out loud; Varney made a real convincing geek.

With Varney gone, there was just my mother to look at, other than the Fabbmobile. She was sitting in a slouch, and she seemed to be staring at her hands, which were clasped real tight together on her knees.

"Do you know what you're going to say to the guy?" I asked her.

Actually, I thought that might be what she was trying to figure out right then, but I couldn't keep my mouth shut and just sit there. I was worried about her, and about me, and about Mr. Fabb, and probably a little about Varney, too; he, at least, would know what he was doing, maybe. But I was especially worried about having no clear idea of what was going to happen next, now that we'd found Mr. Fabb and were, you could say, the only people in the world who could possibly stop him from doing whatever it was he was planning to do.

"Not exactly," she replied. "A lot'll depend on him, how he reacts to seeing me — to seeing *us*. And what he's actually doing. I mean, it looks as if you're right — what you said back at the house. But we don't *know* that yet, for sure. There are still some other possibilities."

I sort of grunted. What was she talking about? Of course I was right. His car being there was proof — his car with padding on the roof for carrying a ladder. How could she doubt my logic, my deductions? Who was Holmes and who was Watson, here?

"Well, if he isn't doing what I said," I said peevishly, "he must be going to do what Dori said." And thinking of that other possibility disrupted all the other thoughts inside my head. At once.

"Or possibly he already *has*," I seemed to have to say, imagining what we would have to do in that case. And pretty sure I wasn't up to any part of it.

"I doubt that Llew has planned to kill himself," my mother said. "I believe what he said in the note — that he doesn't care what happens to himself — but that's a very different thing from *making* something happen. He'd accept the risk involved in blowing up the dome — *that* I can see. He thinks he sees the problem, and he still believes that changes can be made. He's angry and he feels fucked over, but he doesn't feel completely whipped, or powerless, at all."

I probably widened my eyes a little, looking at the back of my mother's head. Her saying "fucked over" like that, to me, told me she was really concentrating. On the problem we faced, but not on form, or the proprieties. As a rule, she doesn't use the f-word, figuratively, while speaking to her impressionable son.

Before I could respond in any other way, the door on the driver's side opened and Varney slid in quickly, closing it behind him. But gently, so it didn't fully latch.

"He's up there," Varney said. He sounded stressed. "Up quite near the top — *you* know, where the stanchion sort of splits in three? He isn't moving,

244

not at all. He's just clinging to the piece he's on, clinging for dear life. I think he's frozen. Christ."

"What?" my mother said. "You mean he's. . . ?"

"*Stuck*," said Varney. "Panicked. You hear about it happening, to newer climbers, mostly. That's a reason not to climb alone. You start to make a move, and then before you finish it, you panic, and you freeze right to the spot. You can't move either way. I'm going to have to go up there and help him." He opened the car door and started out again.

As quickly as he moved, my mother moved as fast, and out the other door. I scrambled after her. I didn't feel appropriate at all. This was the sort of scene that kids like me left to adults to handle. Historically, that is. So far in my life, all stuff like this had been entirely up to them.

Varney had the trunk open again, and by the time I got back there, he'd already taken out some coils of braided nylon rope, stepped into a climbing harness and thrown a sling over one shoulder that had a lot of jingling equipment on it.

He'd also kept on talking.

" . . . give him credit for a plan," he was saying. "He's made it look as if there was a paint job going on, and that he's working for the town. He's got the signs, and buckets, drop cloths — all the different gear."

"How about explosives, though?" my mother said. "Could you tell if he had anything in place, already?"

"No, I couldn't," Varney said. "I couldn't see it, if he has. He's got a backpack on. I think it may be in there, still." He picked up one of the two climbers' hard hats that were in the trunk and put it on his head. "I bet he froze up getting to the place he planned to put the charge." Yes, he had *two* hard hats in the trunk.

"You could use a partner up there, right?" I said. The words came out before I'd thought to say them; I could swear it. "Well, I'm your man, boy, Sherpa, youth — whatever." I reached for the other hat and set it on my head, and at a rakish angle. Of course it was a perfect fit, without adjustment. "Just in case of pigeons, right?" I said, and hee-hawed. All that sounded fake, even to me.

Varney checked my mother out, not me.

"I don't know," he said. "That thing is pretty tall. It *could* be handy, having someone else up there, but it's not essential. Really. Not at all." Mom didn't say a word, and so he switched and looked at me. "How much climbing have you done, exactly?"

"Well, no real *climbing*-climbing, like with harnesses," I said. "Just hand-over-hand stuff, the way you do on Everly. But I've done two outdoor-confidence weekends. So I can tie good knots. And I'm not afraid of heights." The puny ones I'd been on, anyway.

My mother was looking at Varney now.

"It might help Mr. Fabb relax, if he saw Gabe up there," he said to her. "He'd be secure if he came up. Gabe would, I mean. He'd be on a rope that's tied to something solid, all the time."

My mother looked at me and said, "You sure you want to do this?"

It was then, and only then, I knew she wasn't going to stop me — like, *forbid* me. She wasn't going to be my mother in the sense that mother orders, child obeys. She was going to let me make my own decision, based on what I thought I could do (number one), and what I chose to do. No doubt a part of me, inside, was shouting, "Wait! I'm still too *young* to know. *You'd* better say." But another part was saying, "Well, shit. I suppose this had to happen sometime."

That part looked her in the eye and told her, "Yes."

So, with Varney's help, I quickly got another harness on, attached a rope to it, and let him lead me through the trees and over to the stanchion.

As Varney'd said, Llewellyn Fabb had made it look as if a repaint was in progress, using town equipment. The big sectional ladder leaning against the stanchion had "Property of the Town of Dustin" stenciled on the side of it, in orange, and the white canvas drop cloths scattered around the base of it were similarly marked. He'd even gotten "Danger" signs somewhere, and had circled the area with those orange plastic cones. There were extra buckets and some brushes stacked beside the foot of the ladder.

I looked up right away, of course. The top of the ladder, which was a *long* way up, reached the comparative safety of a three-foot-wide metal platform, with a handrail, that completely encircled the stanchion. Going up from there, you climbed on metal rungs (or handholds) that were welded to the side of the stanchion itself, each of them maybe eighteen inches long, and more or less that far apart. These went up and up and *up*, another — what? — perhaps a hundred feet before you got to a second encircling platform, exactly like the first. After that, it was rungs again to still another platform, number three. And a ways above that one — less than fifty feet, I'd say — the stanchion grew three graceful, curving, huge, supporting arms. They spread, and soared and fastened on the edges of the dome itself.

And it was way up there, wrapped tight around the left-hand one, except for just one leg that dangled, drooped, in all that space . . . it was way up there that I beheld Llewellyn Fabb.

I suppose his strategy had been to place his charges on the arms which, being slimmer, would be that much easier to sever, blow apart. He must have shinnied onto one, not thinking, maybe, of the fact that it bent inward from the stanchion. Meaning that a person out on it was over only thin, thin air.

"We'll climb one at a time," Varney was saying. "When I've gotten to the platform and made fast, then you come up. Same thing with the next stretch, and the next one. When we're both on the top platform, I'll rig myself some protection and go out and get a rope around him. Once we've got him safe — secure — it won't be hard to slip this extra harness on." He had it on his sling. "And once we've got him in a harness we can *talk* him off, I'll bet. He'll see that he *can't* fall." Varney made it sound so simple: bim, bam, boom.

"Right," I croaked. I tried to salivate and swallow, but no luck. It was amazing, just the kind of thing you read about in stories. The excitement — no, not fear; *of course* not fear — had dried my mouth out fast as cotton fields back home.

248

My mother, looking rather pale I thought, was chewing on a corner of her lower lip.

"I wonder if *I* shouldn't go up there," she said. *Now* she said it, sure. "Instead of Gabe, I mean. Llew's both my client and my friend, and I'm the one who's meant to know some stuff about the sorts of things you say to people when they're — "

"No," said Varney, interrupting firmly, in his teacher's voice, again. "The things he needs to hear are stuff that has to do with being way up in the sky without a net. He'll need *you* when we get him down. Gabe is stronger; he could be a lot more help, up there." He looked at me. "Let's go."

And that was that. Gabe, that macho-man, the "lot-more-help" . . . he nodded without speaking.

Varney started up the ladder, his equipment making tinkle-clanky sounds. My mother took a step toward me, but checked herself, self-consciously. She smiled, then winked and puckered up her lips, and gave a thumbs-up sign. I grinned at her, or tried to, anyway, then turned and held the ladder while old Varney climbed the thing.

When he got to the platform, he did some quick maneuver with the rope that was also attached to the front of my harness. Then he gave it two quick tugs. I started up.

I'd noticed, watching — *feeling* — it while Varney climbed, that that old ladder sagged and swayed a bit. But I wasn't ready for the way it felt when I was on it. Just about to break? You got it. But of course it wasn't going to. So I told myself. That was just the *feeling* that I had.

I tried to keep from rushing — but neither did I dawdle on that flimsy swaybacked sucker. I consoled myself by thinking that the higher sections, once we left the ladder, would be solid, anyway. Varney kept some gentle pressure on the rope — he'd rigged a pulley on a rung above him — which surely made my climb a good deal easier. I also got the feeling that the harness I had on could really hold me, if it ever had to; that was nice. By the time I reached the platform, my palms had actually stopped sweating, and my body had begun to. I felt more like myself, and a little more excited than afraid.

Varney said, "These next two stretches will be longer." As if I didn't know. "Take your time, and if you feel like resting on the way, that's fine. I've got you all the time." He touched me on the shoulder. "You're doing great," he said. And off he went again, leaving Robin (yes, the Boy Wonder) grinning foolishly behind him.

Watching Varney climb, I had the words "The Human Fly" pop right into my mind and stay there. The guy just swarmed right up the stanchion's side, going at a swift and steady pace, alternating arms and legs so quickly, easily, *mechanically*, it didn't look like work at all.

When my turn came, I found out otherwise almost at once. The metal rungs were round and cold, and because they went straight up instead of tipping slightly forward (as a ladder does), it seemed as if you had to work much harder with your arms to climb. Indeed, your body had this most unnerving tendency to lean a little *backwards* — like, with every step you took.

The rungs were also far enough apart so that your legs felt lots of pressure stepping up, each time. Neither my knees nor those big muscles on the fronts of my thighs were used to being used — *abused* — that way. They soon began to send me messages, like: "Hey, come *on!*" "What *is* this, anyway?" "Easy does it, asshole!" and "Let's take a minute to regroup, okay?" The exercise cliché, "NO PAIN, NO GAIN," in caps, occurred to me. Clearly I was gaining plenty, but of what? Well, *pain*, I thought. *That's great*, I thought. And, *wonderful*. And, *hold on tight* (I thought).

I did stop halfway up that first long straight-up stretch, and at about the same place on the next one, too. Not long. Just long enough to flex the fingers of both hands a half a dozen times, and let the fire in my thighs die down a bit. Boy, if I felt that bad with Varney helping me, I thought, it was even more amazing that Mr. Fabb had gotten that high up, and with a backpack on. Alone, alone, alone.

When I finally reached the third of those small platforms, my legs, particularly in the neighborhood of both kneecaps, were in serious distress. I felt as if the cartilage and ligaments around those useful hinges had been suctioned out somehow, to be replaced by . . . painful air and Jello, maybe. Thinking that a brief massage might help, I tilted forward at the waist and reached in that direction.

Two things happened right away. First, I lost my balance — took a quick step forward with my left foot, even as I grabbed the handrail. And also, I looked down.

Up till then, I hadn't done that once. All my

251

concentration had been focused on two things: pulling inward, going upward. I remembered where I'd been and planned to get back down, eventually. I hadn't felt a need to check and satisfy myself as to my mother's whereabouts. I knew it was a long way up to Mr. Fabb; I'd seen that from the ground.

But when I *did* look down, I found that it was much, much farther than I'd thought. That "a long way up" was absolutely terrifying when it was "a long way down."

I felt the sweat break out on both my palms again, like thin, warm grease, and I began to wipe them on my nonexistent knees. There were these weird sensations on the backs of both my legs and on the bottom of my feet, as if a whole platoon of spiders were, like, creepy-crawling up and down them, only underneath the skin. And finally came a lightness in my head, a reeling sense of having lost control of my ability to move.

"*Gabe!*" said Varney in an undertone, but sharply. He must have seen me, guessed my state of mind, of being. "There is *no* way you can fall. Not now, not ever. Here — look here."

He made me get my head up, focus on my rope, which he had tied around the stanchion. I was about as mobile as a downtown Dustin shopper's tiny poodle, with its leash looped twice around a parking meter.

I sucked a deep breath in, stood up, felt better — even pasted on a sickly (I'm assuming) smile.

Varney nodded and got busy with another rope, then. He ran it through two pulleys that he'd fastened to two rungs. He tied one end of it to his own

252

harness and the other end to the stanchion, and then handed me the coil, the in-between.

"I'm going to go up nearer Mr. Fabb," he said. "Pay the rope out slowly as I go. I'm not going to fall — believe me — but even if I did, you'd be able to pull me back up pretty easily, thanks to these pulleys, here. Hopefully, he'll let me get this other rope around him, pretty soon."

I nodded, looking up at Mr. Fabb. I don't think he'd moved since I'd first seen him. He had his arms wrapped tight around the metal piece that he was on, with his cheek and the front of his body pressed hard against its rounded surface. He was wearing coveralls made of a heavy brown material, with "Town of Dustin" stenciled on the back, in yellow. He also had a blue wool watch cap on his head and black high-top sneakers on his feet. His right foot was jammed into the crotch between the arm that he was on and the middle one, but his left, as I've already said, was simply hanging, dangling in all that space. I couldn't see his eyes from where I was, but I'd have bet that they were squeezed tight shut.

Varney started going up, on rungs much like the ones that we'd been on already. These were still attached to the main stanchion but it, above this platform, started to bend in a little, as I've also said, and get a little slenderer. The last rung — I think there were a dozen of them — was a good six feet below the point that the main stanchion branched into those three long arms (the left-hand one of which, remember, was the one Llewellyn Fabb was clinging to).

When Varney was perhaps three rungs below the

top, he began to speak to Mr. Fabb.

"Mr. Fabb," he said, and I could barely hear him. His voice was gentle, soothing. "This is Varney Poole, a friend of Dori's from the school. You know, her social studies teacher. I've come up to help you; I'm an expert climber and I'm very comfortable up here. Gabe Podesta's with me. He's in a nice safe place a little ways below me, where he can help us, too. And his mother's also with us, on the ground.

"You aren't going to have to do a thing. And I'm not going to do a thing myself, until you're ready for me to. There's a very easy way to get you off there safely; I know exactly what to do. All you have to do is stay right where you are. You're going to be just fine. We're all on your side in this deal. You don't have a thing to worry about."

It was then that the first siren started, far below, to be followed shortly by a bunch of others, and the sound of car horns blowing, everywhere.

And what that made Llewellyn Fabb decide to do was lift his head and open up his eyes and therefore see what-all was going on in town, which was the kind of craziness, I guess, that goes with an evacuation. At least in our hometown, in Dustin.

I'm sure the cops, the firemen and all had tried to make it "orderly," but they had nowhere near the numbers that they needed to inform and regulate the Dustin public. I'm also sure that lots of people did the best thing possible, which was to lock their doors and leave the town by the quickest, shortest route available. But lots and lots of others felt they simply *had to* go the other way, downtown, head right down to their store or office first, and get something or do something, or see something. Still others took it upon themselves to go crosstown and stop at relatives' addresses, to be sure. That meant that very soon a lot of streets were clogged with Volvos and with Porsches, double-parked; pushy little Saabs and Beamers wouldn't wait for lights to change and caused, or were a part of, many accidents. There were some fisticuffs at intersections, and two shootings. Lots of people in my town were acting so completely selfishly that if the dome *had* chanced to fall, they would have caused a lot of most unnecessary deaths including, very possibly, their own.

From far above, where we were, it looked to me (as I've just said) like total craziness, a town gone wild. I don't know what Llewellyn Fabb thought it looked like. But he surely wasn't in the sort of shape — or frame of mind — that's best for thinking logically, or piecing things together.

What he *did*, observed by Varney and myself, was stare at what was happening down there and then, as if repelled (or *activated*, anyway) by what he saw, begin to push himself away from the support that he'd been clutching. It looked as if he planned to sit and straddle it, and slide back down in Varney Poole's direction, and to safety.

Let's say that *was* his plan. But then let's also say that his right foot, which had been jammed for all that time, and on an angle, down in the metal crotch between the arms, had gone to sleep, and so he didn't have control of it. I think that was — I'm pretty *sure* it was — the explanation of what happened next. For when he pulled it out, you see, it didn't drop down over on the far side of the arm, the opposite side from where his left foot had been dangling. No, it came the other way, and so Llewellyn Fabb just dropped right off that arm like someone sliding off a horse.

By then, his head had turned so he could see first Varney — who was leaning, reaching out to him — and then, a little later, me.

I would swear he recognized us both, and I believe he looked completely peaceful and resigned, and maybe even tried to smile. It's possible I had to make that up, in order to get down myself. I heard him land, you see.

31
AFTERWARDS

Dori moved to Jettison City, to her second cousin Justin's, right after the funeral. My parents had told her how much they'd love to have her come and live with us, and I think she believed them, but she also said she couldn't.

"I just couldn't," she repeated and repeated.

She couldn't imagine ever setting foot in Dustin High again; she told me that before she left, by way of partial explanation. She also told me that she felt she'd let her father down.

I tried to make her see that wasn't so, that none of the alternatives — including doing nothing, or swallowing the note — would certainly have helped him, changed the situation. She said we couldn't *know* that, we could only guess. The only thing we *knew* (she said, and started crying) was that what

257

she'd done had turned out dreadfully. She never said she blamed my parents (who, with Varney's help, had worked out all the details of the plan we'd used, remember). Or that Varney and I should have done something different when we had the chance to. But I haven't yet escaped the feeling that she thought those things, had thought them, possibly still did. I've thought that second thing a lot, myself.

At first, right after Dori'd moved up there, I used to call her up and ask her to invite me to her cousin's, or I'd tell her how I'd love it if she'd visit for a day, or spend the night at my place. I'd come and get her, take her back, I said. "Just the two of us," I'd say. "We wouldn't even leave the house." But she kept saying, "No, I can't. Not yet." And after a while, I thought it might be best if I stopped asking. I'd tell her that I loved her and I missed her, and she'd usually say, "I love you, too," but she never said that she'd like to see me. I also wrote her letters, telling her about a lot of what was going on in town, especially the things I thought she'd like to hear.

Dr. Leeds resigned about a fortnight after Mr. Fabb's death, and the other two did also, three days later. The mayor appointed three former school directors to fill the vacancies, pending an election in the spring. My father said he still might run; he hadn't made his mind up yet.

The values classes simply disappeared from the curriculum, though Varney, on his own, decided he would have one final one. It had to do with a bunch of things like loneliness and noticing and caring. I think most people realized it had something to do with Mr. Fabb, and it was probably the best class

Varney'll ever teach in his brief career as a molder of the high school mind. He isn't coming back next year, he's told me; he thinks he may go back to school — to law school, he's been saying lately.

He's been great to me — him and Lafountain, both. I can tell how much they want to help, how much they wish that they could *do* something — for Dori and for me, for all of us. I tell them thanks for being great from time to time, and that they *are* a help, and that they should write her letters, too. I know Lafountain does; Varney may, I'm just not sure.

Mr. Fabb himself has become a far more major, influential figure than he'd ever been in life. He hadn't blown up the dome, or even harmed it, and after a while people started saying that he'd probably changed his mind up there and never would hurt a fly. What he came to represent was, like, a classic "little guy," who really cared about the town and who had served it well, for many years. There were half a dozen serious speeches made at aldermanic meetings concerning low-cost housing in the town — the need for some, that is. That was six more than ever before, and it even looked as if there might be action taken, in the spring. The *Times* ran an editorial concerning Mr. Fabb and the dome, in which it actually called the latter "a mixed blessing, but definitely a blessing," and the school directors tabled (but with an affirmative reaction) a suggestion by the PTA to name the next new school after Llewellyn Fabb.

Me, I've stopped my letters to the school paper. There hasn't been a lot to bitch about, and maybe

259

I'm less . . . motivated than I used to be. Lafountain says he's sure I could be president of the senior class next year, but that's Lafountain for you, right? I have no plans to run, and don't anticipate a draft. My sole ambition is to be with Dori, somehow.

In fact, just yesterday, I raised that possibility, in question form, while talking with my mother.

"Hasn't it been long enough?" I asked her. "How about I simply drive up there one day and ring the doorbell?"

"I don't know," she said. "Grief isn't logical. It doesn't go on any timetable. Everybody's different. In olden days, the nobles used to have a mourning period, when people wore black and didn't go out, even. I think it was six months or something. And only after it was over did they resume their regularly scheduled programs. I guess that that's impractical, today. And besides" — she laughed — "you tell me who the nobles are. But there's something to the principle."

My father, who'd been lurking in the doorway, cleared his throat. I looked at him.

"May I?" he inquired. "Just a tuppence worth?"

"Why not?" I think I even smiled.

"Dori isn't *choosing* this," he said. "It's just what is, for now. She's strong and good; she'll want to see you sometime. She knows that, Gabe, and so do you, deep down, I'm sure. After all, the most important thing between two people is the f-word."

"*What?*" I said. Incredulous. "The *f-word?*"

"Sure," he said, "the f-word. Faith." His eyes were glistening, but now *he* smiled.

And, yeah, I hugged them both, just like it was some sappy sitcom. The simple fact is that the thing I said before is true: I couldn't imagine anyone having a better relationship with their parents than I do.

ABOUT THE AUTHOR

JULIAN F. THOMPSON confesses that he never took a class in values, and he wouldn't want to live in a town located under a dome, either. He prefers Vermont. He and his wife, Polly, who is a painter, printmaker, and designer, live in the northern part in the winter and the southern part in the summer because that's what they feel like doing. His previous novels are *The Grounding of Group 6*, *Facing It*, *A Question of Survival*, *Discontinued*, *A Band of Angels*, *Simon Pure* and *The Taking of Mariasburg*.